JORDAN
VERSION 3.2

A NOVEL

JORDAN
VERSION 3.2

A NOVEL

STACEY COCHRAN

Blank Slate Press | Harrisonville, MO

Blank Slate Press
Harrisonville, MO 64701
Copyright © 2024 Stacey Cochran
All rights reserved.

For information, contact:
info@amphoraepublishing.com

www.amphoraepublishing.com
Blank Slate Press is an imprint of
Amphorae Publishing Group, LLC
www.amphoraepublishing.com

Manufactured in the United States of America
Cover design by Kristina Blank Makansi
Cover art by Oracle Hill Productions LLC
Set in Adobe Caslon Pro, Acumin Variable

Library of Congress Control Number: 2023939480
ISBN: 9781943075812

For Harper and Desmond

"What probability do you put on human inability to control future advanced AI systems causing human extinction or similarly permanent and severe disempowerment of the human species?"

Results: 10% or greater chance that humans go extinct.

—AI Impacts Survey of 738 ML
Researchers from June–August 2022

PART 1

One

When I wake, I am floating in the ocean.

I cough and run my tongue across dry lips, tasting bitter saltwater. My throat is coated with it. I look down and see I'm wearing a yellow inflatable life vest, and from my left shoulder, an emergency locator beacon flashes. The sea stretches endlessly around me and goosebumps prickle my skin, but I don't shiver so long as I keep my arms and legs moving. I look up at the moonless sky teeming with stars and think: Where am I? *Who am I?*

I use my arms and legs to pivot. Floating. Looking for anything. Sign of land. Sign of a boat.

Nothing.

In the bluish starlit tint, I see symbols on the lapel of the life vest. My index finger traces over them.

JOR. V. 3.2
ANAG. NORISIS, INC.

I have no idea what this means.

Two

Midmorning I spot something reflecting sunlight on the water. It glints between the rise and fall of waves. I swim toward it. The swells are four feet from crest to trough. My pants and shirt are made of thin material. Black. Probably loose-fitting when dry, but now they cling to me. My shoes are waterlogged and heavy. My head aches. I draw close to the reflective object.

Some sort of suitcase. Metallic chrome exterior. Watertight. I spin it around. Find a handle and locking clasps on one end. I use it like a buoy for a moment, holding on with both arms. A reflection in the chrome side of the suitcase looks at me.

In the mirror image I see a man, perhaps in his early thirties. Sandy blond hair trimmed close. Lean face. Square jaw. Strong chin. Stubble of a beard. Pale blue eyes. Calm and steady. There's a sharpness in the gaze that looks at me. This is someone with enough heart to see strength in others without it ever diminishing his own. Through the clinging shirt, the outline of muscles on my chest and arms are noticeable. I'm tired, but my legs feel powerful, certainly capable.

•••

A shark passes me in the blue.

I must have fallen asleep. I tied the strap from my life vest to the suitcase handle. The next pass comes a minute later. The shark nudges my knee, causing me to teeter like a cork as adrenaline floods through me.

I try to climb up on the suitcase to get as much of my body out of the water as possible.

No luck.

Moments pass, and all I can think is that I need to get out of the water. I can't see below the surface beyond my waist, but I know the shark is down there, circling me, readying to bite.

From the corner of my eye, I see something floating in the distance.

Just a speck. Bright orange.

Tethered to the suitcase, I swim hard toward the object.

As I approach, I realize the object is a life raft. Round, its diameter is twice my body length. The raft's inflated walls rise above the surface in three tubes stitched on top of each other.

From one side, an emergency exit slide extends like a limb out into the water.

I swim harder.

I reach the side and grab the raft. Pull myself into it.

A teenage boy sits across from me. He stares out at the sea and scarcely seems to notice that I am trying to enter the raft.

"C-c-could you," I ask, "help me?"

The boy, who looks about seventeen or eighteen, has black hair down to his shoulders and dark brown eyes. He wears tan cargo shorts and a tattered button-down shirt open and unbuttoned. A silver canteen rests at his side. He never once looks at me.

"There is," I say, "a shark."

I struggle onboard without his help. Water spills over the side. I pull the suitcase up into my lap and stare at the boy. He says nothing, doesn't even acknowledge my presence.

I then turn and kneel and look out at the ocean behind me searching for the shark.

Three

The boy will not make eye contact, and I realize he is staring into the distance as if something were there. But there's nothing but ocean. I'm strangely moved by him, wondering if the trauma of being alone in a life raft in the middle of...somewhere...has rendered him mute. Or maybe he has some kind of neurological disorder. He appears to be talking to someone else when he finally speaks. "You don't know who you are, do you?"

"No," I say.

"Reality is an illusion," he whispers to himself, "although a very persistent one."

"What're you talking about?" I study him. "You have water in that?" I look at the silver canteen at his side.

Under a cloudless blue sky, the now-sweltering sun is oppressive. The life raft bobs and spins over the undulating waves, and I start to feel queasy. My tongue is scratchy and dry, and it sticks to the roof of my mouth. My head throbs so intensely it makes me disoriented.

"So thirsty," I say.

"Water is made of hydrogen and oxygen. Both are reactive nonmetals."

I reach out my hand. "Would you let me have a drink?"

The boy keeps staring absently out at space and asks, "What are the elemental parts of meaning?"

"Water," I say. "I need water."

His lips move up and down, whispering, but I can't hear him well enough to make out the words. Something about the position of the sun and then, "Radiometric dating suggests the Earth formed four and a half billion years ago."

I stare at him a moment more, then close my eyes and lean back in the raft. I reason through my options, but my thoughts are scattered and frantic.

Finally, I lean forward and try to take the canteen from him. He starts wailing and screaming and clutches the canteen to his chest. "You're trying to kill me!"

"Take it easy," I say. "Just take it easy! It's your water. Your canteen. I'm not trying to kill you."

He cries, his eyes red-rimmed and desperate.

Eventually he soothes himself by rocking back and forth, holding the canteen close to his chest, and whispering things I can't quite hear over the lapping of the waves splashing against the side of the raft.

"Quite a pair," I say. "You and me."

I look around at the interior of the raft, hoping for a pocket of supplies, maybe another canteen, something. But there's nothing. So I kneel again, prop my elbows on the raft's rim, and turn my gaze out at the endless sea.

Four

I jerk awake. The boy is whispering something, talking to himself. Then he laughs.

I swallow hard, my parched throat burning. "These things," I say, turning to face him and pointing to the markings on the lapel of my life vest, "mean something. Someone put them here. I can almost remember."

"Words." He stares at empty space adjacent to the raft.

My gaze drifts to his canteen. "Yes," I say. "Words. You do understand me. They're like pictures of what we say. Words." I look at the markings on the raft: LIFE RAFT, INFLATABLE TWENTY-MAN TYPE F2B. "I just don't know what any of it means."

"Einstein didn't begin talking until the age of four."

"What?" I say, "I don't know who that is. What does that mean?"

"Some people say he had autism," the boy says.

I start to unbuckle my life jacket. "Please, I'll give you this for a drink of water."

He stares at the spot in space, distant from the raft, and then says, "I need water more than I need a life jacket. Besides, I'm in a raft."

"You might need it later," I say. "Who knows where we'll be later."

"We? I'll just wait for you to die."

I stare at him.

He begins whispering to himself again.

I swear, under my breath, then I try calm reasoning. "I can tell you're a kind person. I'm thirsty, and I'm going to die if I don't have a drink of water. Please."

"I know," he says.

"You want me to die in this raft with you?"

He doesn't respond. I study his face and try to recollect having seen it before. Those eyes. Like shards of glass. I ask, "Who are you?"

"I'm no one," he replies.

"You're somebody. Obviously."

"The self is a phenomenal fiction constructed by the default mode network."

"What?"

"Multiple interconnected regions of the brain form the default mode network, which is responsible for memory retrieval, construction of the self, and projection of the self in determining future actions and behaviors."

His mind seems to drift in and out of connection with me, punctuated by flashes of brilliance. For the most part, he seems unaware I'm even in the raft, but then suddenly, he'll say something that makes it clear he *is* aware.

"You don't remember anything either?" I say.

"You going to open that suitcase?" He stares out at space.

"Yes." I don't open it. I've already looked at the lock and am not sure I can open it. "How and why did we come to be here? Do you know who I am?"

"The self is not real," he says. "The self is not an animate thing. Is any human being what they think they are if what they think they are isn't real?"

"I just need a drink of water."

"If someone erases our identities, do we continue being the same person?"

I study his face. "You have no memory either."

"The average human can survive for three weeks without food."

"Will you respond to me?"

"But without water, we all die within days."

"Do you know how we came to be here?"

"Have I seen any signs of a plane crash?" He shakes his head. "Curious. Very curious, indeed."

I consider this, look around the life raft at the endless blue surrounding us. "At least we're alive."

He stares into empty space and taps his lip.

I ask, "What?"

He looks me in the eyes for the first time. I feel like he recognizes me, if only for an instant.

"You know who I am," I say.

He ignores me, turning to look at empty space again, lost once more in his own world.

"Hey," I call. "You recognized me. Just now. You've seen me before."

He rocks back and forth, eyes squeezed shut, clutching the canteen close to his chest.

"Come on," I plead. "I know you can hear me."

He will not engage again. I turn my attention to the suitcase. I try the clasps. "Why would it be locked?"

"Probably food and water inside. I'm sure that's what they put in it."

"They?"

"If we don't know who we are," he says, "we'll never understand why we're here. But can we understand who we are if who we are is not a real thing?"

I stare at him, but he won't meet my eyes.

"You're kind of brilliant," I say. "You know that?"

He points at me but continues gazing at the sea. "Without experiential memory, the default mode network has nothing with which to construct a sense of self. The self becomes nothing."

Suddenly a splintering pain strikes my head from deep within. Everything goes off-kilter, and I find myself on my knees, leaning over the side, coughing and retching into the sea.

Throat raw, I collapse into the raft and clutch at the sides of my head, eyes shut against the light, against the phantom sounds of a woman, screaming, a girl crying.

Two people.

"I need a drink," I say, finally. "Please."

He takes the suitcase from me.

"What're you doing?"

He lifts the case and runs his fingers along the seam where the two halves meet. He eyes it closely.

"I can help you," I say. "We're going to need each other to survive."

His finger taps his lips. "We can't escape who we are."

"I don't know who I am," I say. "I can't remember my name. Or anything else." I shake my head. I sit forward in the raft and gaze from horizon to horizon.

Then he says, "Maybe the reason we're here is to realize we must make our own meaning in life."

Five

I wake that night to a tingly sensation and barely perceptible movement. I slit my eyes open in the starlight and watch the boy slip a knife from the pocket of his shorts. Slowly, he unfolds it until I hear a soft *snick* as it clicks into a locked position. Then he sits, motionless. Watching me. Waiting.

I keep my breathing regular as he creeps forward on his knees, balancing with one hand, trying hard not to make a sound. He holds the knife in his other.

"What're you doing?" I say, my voice rough, thick.

He freezes, stares at me in the starlight, and then, in a crouch, he lunges.

My fist snaps out, landing a brutal uppercut to his jaw, even as his knife slashes across my arm. I feel the cut, yet my skin seems to deflect the blade, as if my flesh were made of leather. The knife falls to the raft floor as the momentum from my blow carries him up and over the edge of the raft.

I grab the knife from the floor and look over the edge to see his fingers scrabbling for traction on the rubber. He tries to climb back in, but I'm not accommodating.

I glare down at him. "You tried to kill me." My forearm is cut and lightly bleeding. I flash the blade at his hands, and he lets go and paddles backward a few feet.

The waves are taller than his head, and he cries out, "I can't swim. I can't swim!"

I pull my shirt off over my head and hold it against the gash across my forearm. Then I reach down and pick up the canteen. I open it and drink, my eyes on him as I swallow.

"Don't drink my water!" he demands. "That's mine."

I watch him treading water. The waves are large enough that I lose sight of him when the raft dips from one to the next.

"Let me back in. I can't swim!" His voice is pleading now.

Clearly he can swim. He seems quite proficient at it. I take another drink from the canteen and slip down to lean against the wet rubber.

Moments later, he starts screaming. "Let me back in! I don't want to die! Let me back in! Please."

I pull myself back up to my knees and watch him sob as the waves buoy him from one dip to the next.

I shrug. "Looks like you're swimming just fine."

"Please."

I lean over the edge, reach out my hand, and help him back into the raft. He scoots to the other side, as far away from me as possible. He holds his hands to his face.

Sometime later in the starlight, he says, "Gratitude is the quality of being thankful, a readiness to show appreciation for and to return kindness."

The canteen rests at my side, the blade still clenched in my hand. I stare at it for a long time, then look up at him. "Look at me," I say. "Look at me when I talk to you!"

The boy's intense gaze holds mine for only the second time. His eyebrows rise, as if he is forcing himself to make eye contact. It's clearly difficult for him.

"Don't do anything like that again. Ever. Do you understand?"

"I am grateful." His voice is a whisper.

I shake my head in dismay. "Do you understand? I won't give you another chance. I'll kill you if I have to defend myself like that again."

The night air has turned cool, and he is shivering, his clothes still wet. He says, "The Bronze Age predated the Iron Age in some areas by as much as one thousand years."

I stare at him and resist swearing. I tried compassion, but now that our tentative trust has been broken, I realize I must be vigilant at all times.

Six

I discover the camera at daybreak.

The sun is rising just above the horizon, and the waves have settled. Despite his wet clothes, the boy has finally started to doze, no doubt from sheer exhaustion.

I don't know what drives my eye to the lens. My first thought is that it's just another grommet, but then, somehow, I know it's part of a camera. I don't know how I know, but I just do. I inspect it. Part of a black rectangular textile panel that adds support in holding the raft's tubes together, the lens is the size of a pencil eraser, and it blends in with the other grommets.

I touch it with my finger. Smooth. Tiny. Half the size of a thumbnail. I touch the other grommets to compare and find they're made of hard plastic.

Three other textile panels around the raft contribute additional support in holding the tubes together. I discover a single lens in each.

Some sort of video archive?

I wave my hand in front of one.

The boy stirs.

"There's a camera lens," I say.

He says nothing. His eyes are red. A bruise has formed along his jaw.

"Look," I say, "in each of these panels."

He sits up and squints into the distance. "Cumulus clouds on the horizon."

A bloom of clouds hangs centrally on the horizon far away. They catch the rising sun's rays from across the ocean and glow gold, orange, and pink. The rest of the sky is cloudless.

"Could be nothing."

"Fixed cumulus clouds in a clear sky at sea indicate land is present," he says.

"How do you know that?"

He whispers to himself and stares at the clouds.

The wind is faint, and the waves are as calm as I've seen since being in the raft. Hard to tell which way the current is moving, but what breeze there is seems to be pushing us in the direction of the clouds.

I track the sun's movement. After a few hours, I stand as well as I can and hold my hand over my forehead to break the sun's glare. I say, "There's land."

He stares out at empty space and says, "Correct."

"Come on."

He shakes his head.

"Wind is pushing us," I say. "But we'll miss it if we don't steer this thing."

He continues shaking his head.

I consider my options. I could force him, threaten him with the knife.

"I really don't want to," he whispers. "Really."

I kneel and pick up my life vest. I put it on over my head. I strap the canteen over my shoulder. "I told you," I say. "I'm not giving you a second chance."

"The tiger shark is a species of requiem shark and the only extant member of the genus Galeocerdo. A large macropredator, it is capable of attaining a length greater than five meters."

"This is ridiculous." I check my pocket for the knife, remove it, secure the life vest, and then climb out of the raft and begin swimming toward land.

I'm a good distance away when he starts yelling repeatedly, "I'll help! I'll help!"

I stop and turn in the water, look back at him in the raft. I grip the knife and stare at the boy, who is trying futilely to stand.

I swim back. "Get in the water and help me kick."

He complies, and we commence kicking and paddling in the direction of land. Eventually, we make progress. We climb back into the raft, exhausted, and I look toward the land.

"The average human can only survive three days with no water," he says.

"So you've said."

He stares at space to the left of my shoulder.

"Thirsty?" I ask.

He nods, and I hand him the canteen and watch him drink.

"Enough," I say. "Give it back."

He hands it back, and I shake it. "You nearly finished it."

"I'm scared."

"Look," I say with a sigh. "You must listen to me, or we'll both die. I'm trying to help you. Understand? I'm trying to help us both survive this."

He nods.

"Tell me you understand."

He stares out at space and says, "I understand."

I turn my attention to the ocean. I gaze around the entire horizon and see no other sign of land or clouds. My mouth is so dry it feels swabbed with cotton. I'm thirsty, hungry, faint, but I will not drink the last of our water. I shake the canteen again and notice my forearm where the knife sliced me. Am I looking at the wrong arm? I glance at the other and see that it, too, is fine. My fingertips trace the spot where the knife cut me. Only the faintest sign of a scar remains.

The boy whispers to himself.

I climb back overboard and resume pushing the raft by kicking and swimming with it through the ocean. He joins me.

Near sunset, I climb back in so I can stand to assess our progress. The boy follows me. A channel separates two islands. The island to my left is smaller. It looks arid and dry, and the tallest hill is steep. The main island is too large to see in its entirety.

I see a strip of sand and palm trees. The hillside looks arid with tan, dry earth and sparse chaparral.

I hand the boy the canteen. "Here."

He glances at it. It is the last of our water.

"It's your water now," he says.

I look at him and compassion wells up in me once more. Maybe it's that I see a lot of myself in him. We're both ruined in our own ways, me with no memory of who I am, him without the social or emotional skills necessary to cooperate. To survive. I feel the need to take care of him, help him. Protect him.

"Come on," I say. "We're almost there."

We climb overboard and resume pushing the raft. Soon the sun goes below the ocean's horizon.

The two of us hold onto the raft on opposite sides of the exit chute and kick in unison toward the main island. The sound of breakers crashes over a reef in the distance. The waves pick up quite a bit. The water is deep. Stars speckle the sky.

Suddenly the boy disappears underwater.

He surfaces a moment later, only to disappear again. Then I see an arm, then two. Flailing at the water. Thrashing. Screaming.

I kick as hard as I can and make contact with something that moves quickly away. Then I move behind the boy and push him up into the raft, climbing up after him. Blood smears the rubber and begins to pool in the raft as the boy clutches his side. Something has taken a piece of him. He starts to shake, hyperventilating and in shock. His eyes are wide with fear.

"Hang on! We're almost there. We can get help." I stroke his long hair back from his face. "Don't close your eyes. Hang on! Come on now, kid! Keep your eyes open!"

His face is pale. I grip his hand, and his fingers close around mine. He looks up at me, gasping. "I don't. Remember. Who I. Am. *Either.*"

His eyes glaze over, a smile forming on his lips. His hand goes limp, fingers loosening their grip.

"Open your eyes! Come on! Open your eyes! I'm gonna take care of you! You're going to be alright! Open your eyes! Don't go to sleep! Come on, kid. I'm with you. You're not alone."

A moment later, a breaking wave crashes over the side of the raft, filling it with water. The raft grounds on the reef not far from the beach.

"Help!" I yell toward land. "Help! Somebody, please!" I cradle the boy's head. "Open your eyes. Please!"

Another wave strikes us, snagging the raft more firmly on the coral. I tumble overboard and push off against the reef, dragging the raft toward the beach.

I swim and push along the bottom with the raft tailing behind me, slowly deflating. Once I've got it out of the surf, I grab the boy and drag him further up onto the sand. His body is heavy. I drop to my knees and put my ear near his mouth. Listening for any sign of breathing. Put my ear to his chest.

No heartbeat. No breathing.

I stare at him for a while. Touch his face. No response.

I look up and down the beach searching for any sign of civilization.

"Help! Anyone! Help!"

Seven

Covered in the dead boy's blood, I remove my life vest, throw it aside, and stagger back toward the water, which shimmers in the moonlight under a sea of stars. I fall to my knees at the shoreline.

Shaken.

I listen to the roar of the breakers and reach down into the wet sand, relishing the feel of it, letting it lave through my fingers. The breeze coming in from the sea is soft, and I raise my face to it.

That's when I see the chrome metal briefcase wash ashore. It must have gone overboard when we hit the waves near the reef. I gaze at it in the moonlight before looking back down at the surf. Then I go to work rinsing the boy's blood from my body.

Breathe, I tell myself. Breathe.

Finally, I stand, grab the briefcase handle, and return to the boy—more a young man really. I pick him up by the armpits and pull him toward the edge of the beach under a row of palm trees. I arrange his arms and legs so he looks comfortable even though I know it doesn't matter. Then I retrieve the briefcase and sink down into the sand beside the boy. I peer out at the lagoon and the breaking waves on the reef. Behind me, the land smells swampy, brackish. Because of the darkness, thick undergrowth, and trees, I can't see far.

I remove the canteen strapped over my shoulder. Open the cap. Think about it for a moment, then tilt my head back and savor the final drops. After replacing the cap, I pat my pocket and feel the knife locked in its casing. I remove it. Open the blade. Look at it.

I consider my situation.

A suitcase that won't open, an empty canteen, a destroyed raft, a knife, a life vest, and the soaking wet clothes that I wear. These are my possessions. I have no clear memory from before two days ago. The only other person I know just died in my arms. The island appears uninhabited. It occurs to me that were I to ruminate on these things too long, my mind could easily move to thoughts as dark as storm clouds.

I pick up a handful of sand, fling it as hard as I can, and yell at the stars in the night sky.

Eight

Near daybreak I go to work on the raft with the knife. Rigor mortis has set into the boy's body, and flies swarm him. I know I will have to bury him soon or abandon him on the beach and begin a search of the island's interior.

I cut into the rubber material surrounding the black textile panel. Tough, but the knife performs well and a minute later I insert my hand inside the tube and find the small camera behind the panel.

I wrench it free.

The camera is the size of a coin, weighs only an ounce, and the lens extends from a small tube. I find no lights or buttons powering it, and I hear no moving parts inside.

I stare at it for a long time.

"Can you hear me?" I ask. "Is anyone there?"

Nothing indicates a reply, so I go to work on the other lenses.

•••

With the cameras removed from the raft, I focus my attention on the chrome suitcase. It has no markings or symbols like those on the life vest and raft. I try prying it open with the knife. That quickly proves futile, and I risk cutting myself as the blade slides off the metal. Perhaps I can bash open the locking clasps with a rock. Hands on my hips, I look around. No rocks.

Out of options, I turn my attention to the boy. I decide to bury him on the edge of the beach, and after digging a shallow trench with my hands, I roll him into it and push sand over him. I gather palm fronds and driftwood and place them over the mound to mark his grave.

Nine

I set out after sunrise through the swampy interior, taking only the knife and empty canteen. I leave the suitcase, life vest, and destroyed raft. I glance back one last time at the boy's sandy grave, the stones and driftwood atop the narrow mound.

Then I turn away and face the darkness. The flora is dense and brambly around me. The sand, below a foot of brackish water, sucks at my feet. Mosquitoes cloud around me, but swatting them away from my face does no good. In places, the thick branches are like chitinous webs, and I stumble and fall more than once trying to part them.

I soon come into a clearing. I climb up out of the forest through a dusty ravine that rises to a saddle-shaped pass. I glance back over the trees to the reef and ocean beyond. The hills to either side are covered in cacti and thorny shrubs. I continue up the ravine, sweating and out of breath. Below my feet, the ground is hard, volcanic.

I worry about snakes.

Eventually, I arrive at the pass and see both sides of the island. The interior continues to my left up the ridgeline, but the immediate hill blocks my view.

I look back in the direction I came and see the beach beyond the swamp and reef. Lines of white breakers hit the coral, marking the divide between lagoon and ocean. I glance at my forearm. Now even the faintest trace of a scar is gone. It looks as though I'd never been cut.

The smaller island across the channel rises steeply from the ocean. A white sand beach skirts some of its shoreline, but steep cliffs comprise most of its coast.

I see no other sign of land, and my view to the north, west, and south is far.

It makes little sense to continue down the opposite side of the pass because I can see the coastline. The unknown is the island's interior up the immediate hill from the pass.

I begin to climb it.

My heart beats hard in my chest. My breathing is deep and steady, pulling oxygen into my lungs. I scramble up a steep grade and arrive at a peak.

The interior sprawls before me.

The spine of the island is a long ridgeline. A few other peaks rise in the distance higher than where I stand, but the prominence is enough to reveal an end to the island, and beyond that the blue of the ocean sparkles and dances in the sunlight.

Using the sun's position low in the morning sky, I reason through the geography in terms of north, west, south, and east. The ridgeline dips down to a valley at the island's midpoint and then rises again on the eastern end and forks into two diverging ridges. The interior of the fork cradles a large natural harbor.

Two features draw my attention.

First, the distant hill near the split in the fork appears a rich shade of green. It stands out noticeably from the rocky outcroppings and arid shrubbery covering the rest of the island.

Second, I spy a thin trail of smoke rising into the sky from somewhere along the harbor in between the split.

Ten

Midmorning. I'm walking along the valley's arroyo when I spot a young woman on a rocky outcropping inland from the beach. I use my hand like a visor to cut the sun's glare. Tanned and wearing clothes the color of sand, she's camouflaged well against the arid hillside. Graceful and stealthy, she moves like a predator. I wave and call to her, but she vanishes into the scrub.

"Hey!" I call out again, waving frantically. But she doesn't reappear. Maybe she was a mirage. I'm so disoriented from thirst and hunger, I question whether I've seen anyone at all.

I continue eastward and after another half hour, I realize the ground is damp and muddy. I keep going until I see water. First small puddles, then larger pools.

I drop to my knees. Hands shaking, I drink in big mouthfuls, cupping the water with my palms, not caring that it tastes of dirt.

Finally sated, I stretch out in it. Salt rinses off my body, mud sloughs off my shoes, and the scent of the dead boy washes away.

I uncap and hold the canteen under the surface to refill it, then go still. Whispers. Slowly I recap the canteen and listen. There it is again. My head snaps around toward a cluster of trees. No movement. No one there. I think of her, slinking across the rocks.

"Are you there?" I might be talking to myself, but I still ask.

There's no reply.

Eventually, I rise to my feet, take a long look ahead of me, and begin walking again.

The pools grow larger and better connected until they resemble a flowing stream over the rocks.

As the water grows more abundant, the vegetation flourishes along the banks and extends farther away from the creek.

Small acacia and mesquite give way to riparian woodland. The branches catch the breeze coming down from the eastern hill ahead, and the green leaves rustle in the wind. Grass and reeds cover the bank, and the shade cools my skin.

The water is clearer here. I drink from it until my throat no longer burns from dryness.

I empty my canteen and refill it. Crouching, I splash my face and glance up at the treeline. I'm hungry to the point of weakness, dizziness, but still I sense movement among the trees.

I freeze.

"Who are you?" she calls from across the creek.

I look up from the pool. She has a spear trained on my chest. Her face is dirty, but her eyes are sharp. Pale green. I've seen green like that before. Long legs end at a pair of shorts and a tank top that's dirty with sand and mud.

The spear is fashioned from a five-foot length of gray steel pipe. The end is sharpened to a point, and there're signs of blood on it. She wears a knife in a leather sheath tied to her hip, but the spear aimed at my chest holds my attention. I consider making a play for the knife in my pocket, but she reads my movement and says, "Keep your hands where I can see them."

I slowly raise my arms, palms toward her, so she can see my hands are empty.

"Do you know your name?"

I clear my throat. "No."

She tilts her head, closes one eye, sighting me down the length of the spear.

"I have no memory prior to three days ago. I think I was in a plane crash."

25

No reply. She is studying me now. Her eyes move over me: my hair, forehead, eyebrows, and eyes. My mouth. Then her gaze moves over my neck and chest, and she squints. She glances at my waist and thighs, and her eyes shoot back to mine. She scowls.

"I washed ashore last night with a kid who is dead. A shark bit him. Bad. About a half mile out, at the reef as we were approaching the island. He bled to death on the beach."

She remains silent, targeting me from a throwing position.

"Please," I whisper.

She sights me a moment longer, then raises her head and holds my gaze. "Never forget I let you live here today. Others would kill you. Eat you."

I say nothing.

"Do you understand?"

I don't understand. Not at all. But I believe her conviction. "Yes."

Our eyes remain locked on one another.

"Drink," she says. "But make it fast. You don't want to stay here long."

"Who are you? What's your name? Where am I?"

She lowers the spear and looks upstream as though searching for movement. "Drink."

"What are you—"

"Drink."

"What are you looking for?"

She gives me a long steady look from the bank, eyes clear and focused, eyebrows level. Her lips are a thin line. The tree branches rustle upstream on the wind.

"Death," she says. "Now drink before it comes for us."

I kneel and drink and wash my face. Water drips from my grizzled chin. I wipe at it with my forearm, never taking my eyes off her for long. I can't tell whether she wants to hurt me or help me. I keep my guard up.

"I've not eaten in three days," I say.

She looks into my eyes with pity. She reaches into a pocket, removes something, and throws it at me square in the chest. Some kind of salted meat, wrapped in seaweed. Kelp. I taste it. Salty, tough, redolent of the sea. I devour it.

"I don't remember anything."

She glares at me as if studying a poisonous snake from a safe distance.

"Where are we?" I ask again.

"They've started—modifying—new arrivals. They want to see if you can survive. They want to see if I can survive you."

"They who?"

She says, "You're going to have to give me the knife."

"What knife?"

She frowns. "That's not a good way to establish trust. You want to survive?"

She drops down from the bank, not more than three feet from me, and fills a leather bota with water. She drinks. Then she rises, slings it over her shoulder, and looks into my eyes.

Before I have time to react, she jams her spear into the ground, whisks her knife from its leather sheath, and presses it against my throat. I make a play for my knife, but she grabs my forearm. Her grip is strong, talon-like.

With her body pressed firmly against mine, caging me, she leans in close to my ear and whispers, "*You.*" She takes one small step back. "Give me the knife."

"What knife?" Her blade presses deeper into my flesh. I let out a grunt of shock.

"I'll bleed you right here. Right now."

She stares into my eyes. I believe her. I slowly remove the knife from my pocket.

"How did you know?" I ask.

Her grip loosens, slides down my arm, and takes the folded knife from my hand. Her pale green eyes have flecks of brown around the edges. Freckles spot her nose. Her lips are full and pale pink. An intense wave of attraction comes over me.

"Kinda hard to miss," she says, "in those pants."

She glances at my waistband. Her eyes drop down the length of my legs before she puts the knife into her pocket. She finally removes her knife from the side of my neck.

She grabs the spear. She looks into my eyes once more. She shakes her head and spits.

"What?" I ask.

She returns her knife to its sheath before darting up the bank.

"Come on," she says. "If they want me to play along, let's see what you're made of."

Eleven

She leads me away from the water and toward the arid hills to the north, stopping frequently to scan the periphery. She says nothing and doesn't respond to anything I say. Her pace quickens, and when we come over a hill, I see the rocky coastline far below.

Soon we approach a sandstone cliff that drops far down to the ocean. At places the hillside cuts inward beyond vertical.

"Where are we going?" The cliffs look unstable and impossible to descend.

"You can turn back now and try your luck inland," she says, "with the others."

"I'm just asking. Where are we going?"

"Somewhere safe." She fastens her spear through a series of leather straps tied to the bota slung over her back and then follows a narrow path through scrubby cliffside vegetation. We reach a point where there is no way down.

"There are only a few spots," she says, turning and sizing me up from head to toe, "that are really dangerous."

"You're not going to climb down this cliff."

She lifts a rock that must be twice her weight. Her lean muscles strain against the effort, and a light sheen of sweat beads around her neck. A drop slips free and traces down her chest, disappearing into her cleavage. I force myself to look away.

From a hole beneath the rock, she grabs a rope with one hand, then grunts and drops the rock back into place.

"*We* are going to climb down this cliff. Together."

"Wait, what?"

"Yucca." She holds up the rope.

"'Yucca'?"

"Just follow what I do." She places a loop at one end around the rock, tugs at it to make sure it is secure. She studies me again. "Closely."

"Wait. You want me to climb down this cliff on a hand-woven rope?"

She glances at the woods again. "You don't know anything about this island. If you want to live, you'll follow me."

"What are we in danger from? I haven't seen a single threat on this island outside of your spear. What are you so afraid of? Help me understand."

"There are two tribes on this island, one of which would like to see me dead. I can explain more once we reach safety, but we're exposed standing out here. And so, I need you to pay close attention to what I'm about to tell you. There's a ledge about six body lengths down."

"You made this?" I motion at the rope, which appears frayed and made of plant-like material.

"Yes. Now watch me."

I glance at the thin fibers. "No way this will hold my weight."

"It will hold, and you are not a coward," she says as a matter of fact. And she is right. I may not remember my past, but I'm not as afraid as I probably should be. Or maybe it's that she's so confident. Strong. Undeniably sexy. An excitement builds in my chest, vibrating like the pull of a bow across a violin string, and that is enough to make me want to follow her down the rope.

"That's a long fall," I say, mostly to myself to try and talk myself out of this.

"Duly noted."

I want to be with her...wherever we're going. "I'll watch you."

She turns to glance at me, an odd look on her face. Dropping the rope, she steps toward me and grabs both of my shoulders. Our bodies a whisper away from touching. My pulse races. Her scent of earth and exertion is intoxicating. I need food. Her body is making me dizzy. Her hand reaches up and cradles my face. As much as I want to lean into her hand, I feel myself pulling back. This must be some sort of test.

"What are you doing?" I whisper, chastising myself for taking a step away from her.

"Nothing," she says, a small grin on her lips. "Just seeing how you handled tight quarters."

I want to kiss her. Instead I pick up the rope and say, "You're crazy."

"Crazy enough to survive this place longer than anyone else."

She reaches out to take the rope away from me, her hand lingering longer than necessary, and I feel myself breathing her in for a moment. She withdraws before I can take a second breath, and she glances down at my midsection. Her eyes narrow.

"What?"

Without warning, her hands are around my torso, bringing her body dangerously close to mine.

"What are you doing?" I say, trying to keep my voice calm despite her proximity.

"Once I'm down there, I'll give the rope a tug and you pull it up and tie it around your waist like this." Glancing down, I notice that she is not hugging me but rather tying the rope around my midsection, pulling it snug at the navel. "Tie it just as I do before lowering yourself down or you'll plummet to your death."

My face shifts into a frown. "I know how to tie a bowline knot."

Her eyes shoot up to mine. "You remember that?"

"Hmm... I guess I do." I hear the wonder in my tone. "My name or how I got here, not a clue, but knot tying my brain seems to recall. Wonderful."

"Tying a knot will save your ass faster out here than knowing your name."

Holding my gaze, she undresses the knot she just fastened and the attraction builds in me again. What is it about this woman that makes me react so viscerally? Yes, she is beautiful, but surely, I've been around beautiful women before. Perhaps it's her rugged sensuality, the way she looks at me, sharp-eyed and confident, combined with her obvious courage and know-how. And she doesn't want to kill and eat me. At least not now.

Whatever it is, I am completely turned on by her, and I'll follow her anywhere she wants me to go.

With lightning speed, she has the rope around her own waist and is standing on the edge of the cliff.

"Wait." I take a step forward. "I feel like I should go first. To make sure the rope will hold."

She throws me a death glare. "Really? You're going to go all chivalrous on me and play the Man Card? Look, I've done this a thousand times. You're the one who needs my help," she says. "Not the other way around. The sooner you get that through your head, the better."

Pulling the fibers taut against the rock to which it is secured, she leans her body away from the cliff's edge, pushes off, and disappears. Cautiously, I approach the edge and lean over to watch her descend. She looks up at me. Sweat drips from her temples. "Watch and repeat! Do *exactly* as I do."

I nod, vowing to commit her every movement to memory. With her feet, she pushes out away from the cliff. In mid-swing, she quickly slides down the rope about five or six feet. The rocky tide pools shimmer far below. One miscalculation or tear of the woven fibers and she'll be a goner. The rope beside me creaks but holds her weight. Her pendulum arc brings her back toward the cliff, and a millisecond later she disappears into the sandstone.

For a moment, I panic. Did she make it?

No sooner have I thought the worst when I feel a tug of the rope and then it swings freely in the air.

"Your turn!" she calls from a place beyond where I can see her.

Adrenaline trills my heart. I can barely breathe, but I know there really is no other option. She's right. I don't know this island. I don't know the dangers. All I know is that if I want to live, she's my best bet. Taking a deep breath, I drink from the canteen before securing it on my strap. I pull at the rope attached to the rock. I'm not convinced it will hold my weight. She is two-thirds my size.

"I can't do this."

Just then a screech of a bird comes from the woods, startling me. Something moves in the shadows and suddenly it doesn't matter if I don't believe whether I can scale down a cliff or not. I *have* to.

Yanking the rope, upward I secure it around me, knotting myself in faster than I'd have thought possible. Without further hesitation, I lean backward, just as she did, and hand over fist, lower my body along the fibrous braiding, praying silently for it to stay secure.

Glancing up at the cliff, I keep waiting for some sort of beast or weapon to peer over the edge and send me plummeting to my death. When my feet hit the ledge, I nearly jump out of my skin. Swallowing down my fear, I push back away from it as she did and then realize, much too late, that I did not begin my descent fast enough. I am about to swing back straight into the ledge.

A hand jets out of the shadows, grabbing my leg and yanks me toward her. I come crashing down and into her body as we collapse into a heap on the edge of an alcove.

"You idiot!" she hisses, pushing me off her. "You were supposed to lower yourself *as* you swung. Not after."

"I know," I gasp, placing my hand over my beating heart. "I panicked. I heard a noise from the woods." My heart beats like a timpani drum in my ears as my breath fights to steady itself. "Sorry."

"What kind of noise?" she asks, glancing at the earth above her as though whatever threat was up there might be making its way to us.

"A bird. Then, a rustling came from the woods."

At that, she frowns. "Pity. That could have been lunch. Feral chicken. Or quail." She stands up and dusts herself off. There is a bit of blood against her arm from where she braced my fall.

"You're hurt," I say, standing up.

She glances down at where I'm looking. "It's nothing." She grabs her spear from off the ground and waves her hand. "Come on. The next few drops aren't so bad."

"There's more?" I gasp, looking into her eyes. "Why would you live down here? This is insane."

"Because others on this island will cut your throat," she says. "Plus the view's not half bad."

"The view?"

"Now, can you stay right here and not get yourself killed?"

"Where are you going?"

"I need to hide this thing beneath the rock." She pulls at the line. "I don't ordinarily use it for climbing but rather for tying up bundles of wood to lower down the cliff."

"Oh, now you tell me," I say. "So, then how're you getting back down?"

She looks straight into my eyes, smirks just enough to be sexy, and says, "I don't need a rope."

Twelve

"It's pretty easy from here." She dangles by one hand from the escarpment above the alcove, the rope now gone, and then swings and drops to her feet adroitly on the narrow ledge where I've been huddled waiting for her return.

"Easy?"

She refastens her spear at her shoulder. "Follow me."

She leads me along a narrow, ledged path like a catwalk carved into the side of the cliff. At points the path is little more than tree-branch width, and fissures in the sandstone suggest instability and impermanence. The wind blowing in from the ocean and up from the rocky tide pools below flutters my shirt and pants legs.

Eventually, we come to a cave with a view out over the sea. The waves below crash against the rocks. The smell of marine decay is strong, the sound of the surf constant.

"How's your head?"

"I'm fine. Just bumped it a little bit when you pulled me into the alcove."

She comes close and fingers my scalp. "Fascinating."

"What?"

"Give me your arm."

I hold out my arm, and she grips it. Pokes and prods at it.

"What is it?"

"Let me see your neck," she says. "Your back." She pulls up my shirt and fingers my vertebrae from my shoulder blades up to the base of my skull. She feels my collarbone. She slides her fingers to my lower back just above my sacrum.

"Hey." I wriggle away from her, turn to face her. "What are you doing?"

She studies me, her eyes processing things I can only guess at. She stands her spear on the floor, leaning it against the wall. "You're hungry."

"I have no idea when I last had anything resembling a real meal. At least three days." I hold a trembling hand out in front of me. "I can't stop shaking."

She cuts a strip of dried meat from a hindquarter hanging from a slab of wood jammed between the walls of the cave near the ceiling. Kelp leaves hang from a twine strung underneath the beam. She wraps the meat slice with kelp and hands it to me.

"Eat."

I do. And I watch her.

Those pale green eyes with flecks of brown around the edges. Alert. Quick and intelligent. Shaded with an edge—a darkness.

Yet when she glances at me now, I believe I see compassion in the way her gaze darts at me but only for an instant. And in the slight smile on her lips. She's about my age, maybe a year older.

She steps deeper into the cave, and I notice a makeshift cask, square and lined with animal hide. From the ceiling, water drips from the sandstone into the cask. She scoops a cut gourd into it, drinks it all in one long gulp, and then refills her bota.

"You're lucky to have survived," she says.

I look from her to the cask. Nod. "What is that?"

"Sandstone," she says, pointing at the ceiling. "Filters the water."

"You can drink it?"

"Yes." She looks at the nearly finished meat in my hand. "More?"

"I thought I was going to die."

"We all die." She cuts another piece and wraps it in a kelp leaf for me. "But how many of us really live—or even know who we are?"

As I eat, I look around the cave. Drink water from my canteen. Notice stacks of driftwood, cordage, a fire ring, plants hanging from a twine of "yucca" as she calls it, a stump of wood, a mortar and pestle.

"Want me to top that off?" she asks.

I nod. She takes the canteen from me and pours water from the cask into it until full. Hands it back to me.

I am silent for a long time.

"What is this place?"

"No one knows. Some think they know. But they don't." She shakes her head, and her look grows distant. "Everyone arrives by sea, says they've been in a plane crash. Some say they remember a big explosion, a big bang, but nobody remembers anything from before that."

"I don't remember anything," I say, "from before."

"Nobody does. Not consciously anyways."

"How many people are there?"

"On the island?"

I nod.

"Maybe close to fifty. Still alive."

"You called them 'the others' before."

"You'll find out soon enough," she says.

"Does it come back?"

"Your memory?"

I nod. She shakes her head and sighs. "No."

"Any phones? Boats?"

"You're not understanding."

"I'm trying to."

"No phones," she says. "No boats."

"Okay."

"A few have tried to leave. No one ever comes back."

"Maybe they found land."

"And told no one about this place?" she says. "Sent no one back for the rest of us? Think about that."

I run a hand down my face. "But people have left?"

"And were likely killed at sea."

"You don't know that, though."

"I'm saying to you no one has ever returned after escaping."

I think about it. Then ask, "And no one knows who they are or why they're here?"

She looks into my eyes, says nothing. Her eyes say it all.

"Do we even know where we are?" I ask.

She doesn't reply.

"Surely boats must pass by here."

She cuts a piece of meat for herself, wraps it in a kelp leaf, then eats.

"What about airplanes?" I ask. "A signal fire to catch their attention?"

"I've been here longer than anyone else. Not once has an airplane crossed these skies."

"What is your name?" I ask.

"It doesn't matter."

"What can I call you?"

"I'm no one."

"I can't just call you 'no one.'"

"I call myself 'Aleah,' but—" She pauses a long while, looking into my eyes as though searching for something—or deciding whether she wants to trust me. "I'm just like all the others. Just like you. I can't remember anything from before the island either."

"Then we are truly lost."

"Or truly free." She frowns and holds my gaze. "We need a name for you."

"You decide," I say.

"It's your name, new arrival."

"I'm curious what you'd come up with."

We look at one another for a long time. I almost believe she doesn't hate me. She says, "How about 'Jordan'?"

"'Jordan'?"

"Yes."

"Why 'Jordan'?"

"It suits you," she says.

"Jordan," I say. "I don't feel like a Jordan."

She smiles. We share a moment. A connection has been made, though I'd be hard-pressed to explain what exactly that means.

I could almost believe we're flirting.

"How long have you been here?"

She shrugs. "I don't keep track of time anymore."

"But if you did?"

"Years."

I remain quiet for a long time, considering everything she's told me. Eventually I ask, "Why did you help me?"

"I almost killed you," she says. "Twice."

"But you didn't."

"I still might."

I don't doubt that she could. Still, I press, "Why didn't you?"

"You going to keep asking me questions?"

"You rather I didn't?"

"That was a question."

"Was it?"

She smiles, green eyes gleaming. "I should've killed you."

Thirteen

At dusk, Aleah takes a coil of yucca rope from beside a stack of driftwood inside the cave. She measures a section the length of her hand and places it on the stump near the cave entrance. With her knife, she cuts the piece. She coils the bulk and puts it back inside the cave near the woodpile.

"What're you doing?" I ask.

"Watch closely."

She unravels the cut piece of rope with her fingertips, separating the tiny hairlike strands into a bundle the size of a bird's nest. She pulls at the bundle to broaden it and puff it out a bit. It looks very dry.

Next she gathers a handful of twigs from beside the woodpile, and she places them atop the stump beside the nest she's made. She glances at me, then uses her knife to pin the nest to the stump. From the ground, she grabs a piece of rock.

"Flint," she says. "You can find this in the creek bed."

Holding the knife embedded in the nest, she strikes the back of the blade with the flint. It takes her exactly five strikes before a spark takes hold. She blows gently on it, and a flame comes to life. She drops the burning nest of dried yucca threads into the stone fire ring and then places the twigs on top of it one at a time.

She breathes on it a few more times until a steady blaze crackles and smokes. She grabs some of the driftwood.

"You find a rhythm," she says.

"I'm grateful, Aleah. To you. For this."

She continues back and forth between the fire and stack of wood until she's satisfied.

"I found cameras on the raft." I wait for her reaction. She doesn't respond and appears not to have heard me. She stands by the fire, assessing its status.

"Strange," I say. "Best I can figure, they were recording us for some reason. Four lenses. Four tiny cameras."

She glances at me.

I continue, "Why would anyone record what goes on in the raft?"

She grows silent. After some time, she says, "Enough for tonight. I don't want to talk anymore."

"Why not?"

"I'm tired. You'll learn more, new arrival—"

"Jordan."

"You like it." She offers me a blanket. I take it from her. Our fingers touch, and she looks at me. "We have nothing but time on this island."

I lie down on the dirt floor of the cave and gaze at the glowing embers.

The smell of smoke.

Water dripping into the nearly full cask.

Surf crashing on the rocks below.

Fourteen

I wake with a start as though shocked with a bolt of electricity. Sit upright and look around in the darkness.

Where am I?

Am I awake? My skin is damp with cold sweat. Think I might still be asleep, and this is a dream within a dream.

"Hello?" I whisper.

No reply.

Alone.

There was a child in the dream. A girl.

Young.

She was in a white room.

Something had been chasing her away from me. I'd wanted to help. An explosion had brought the dream to an intense end.

"Hey," I say in the darkness. "Aleah."

No reply. I remove the blanket and retrieve my canteen. I stand and walk toward the opening of the cave.

I look out over the ocean glimmering in the moonlight.

My mouth is dry, and a breeze sweeps over the cliff outside the cave. I sip from the canteen.

I look back in the cave, now more awake, and call, "Aleah? You there?"

No reply.

Movement on the rocks below catches my attention. Forty feet down the cliffs.

A ledge of rock stands at a height that allows the taller waves to spill over the top where it fills crevices, creating tide pools. I see a figure in the darkness.

Dark as charcoal in the moonlight, she holds the spear. She is naked.

I watch, transfixed.

She wades out into the pool. The water comes up to her knees. She freezes and then jabs.

She pulls it up, and a crab wriggles on the tip. She climbs from the pool and carries the spear and crab over to a flat-topped boulder. She works for a moment.

Then she vanishes into the cliffs below.

I lean out to see her and nearly lose my balance and fall over the edge. I right myself, swear, and then step back toward the safety of the mouth of the cave.

The dying embers warm my skin.

Aleah emerges over a ledge to my right a few minutes later. She carries twine tied to three large crabs, a fish the length of her forearm, and a string of kelp leaves.

Beautiful.

She looks up at me, then approaches and holds out the twine for me to take. "Breakfast," she says. I take her offering, and she walks past me into the cave.

Wordlessly, I watch her and then look down at the fish, crabs, and kelp.

Enough to feed us both for a day.

Fifteen

Licking her fingers, Aleah glances at me. "Last night you said you saw a camera on the raft."

I look at her across the fire. Her skin glows in the light of the flickering embers, and I fight down a sudden urge to kiss her. She is that striking. Shaking my head to clear my thoughts, I refocus. "I did," I say. "Four of them were mounted inside the raft. Tiny lenses. Like grommets."

Her eyes glance from the remains of breakfast out to the ocean, distant from the cave's mouth. "If you survive, it won't be the last you see."

"Yeah?"

"They're everywhere."

"Cameras?"

She nods, glances at me. I study her expression. She wipes her mouth. "Hundreds," she says. "Thousands even. Tiny. You find them from time to time. Hidden."

"What the hell?"

"No one knows who put them here or why."

"You're telling me this island is rigged with—"

"Yes."

"Who?"

"No one knows," she says. "One of the groups—tribes, I call them now—has developed a belief system based on the watchers, filled with rules and punishments for how to behave. If we do this, it will please the watchers. If we do otherwise, they will punish us."

I grow silent and eye my surroundings closely. The entrance to the cave, the ledge, the hillside.

"Here?" I ask.

She retrieves something from near the cask, opens her palm for me to see. Three small cameras not unlike the ones I'd found on the raft. They've been smashed with a rock.

"I've scoured every square inch around the mouth of this cave. There are probably others. I destroyed these long ago."

"How deep is the cave?"

"Something you should know about me, Jordan," she says. "I choose to behave as though I'm being watched at all times."

"What does that even mean?" I rub the back of my neck, wondering how all this could be real.

"It means exactly what I just said it means."

"Why are you telling me all this?"

She looks into my eyes for a long time. She sighs. "There are things you should know."

"Things?"

"Things I wish I'd known."

"Tell me something," I say. "Why should I trust you?"

"What else are you going to do?"

"Not trust you."

Her mouth twists into a knowing smile. "That would be unwise."

"Maybe so."

"You need to understand," she says. "Once you leave this cave, this hillside, you're being watched at all times."

"Does it matter?"

"That someone erased your memory, sent you here, and is watching you?"

"That's not what I meant."

"What then?" Her voice is tinged with exasperation.

"What difference does it make to me? Am I going to act differently knowing that?"

She looks at me in a way that I interpret as a mix of pity forged by understanding.

"The knowledge that there is someone out there," she says, "'someone' or 'something' that could rescue us, an entity that cares about what we do and how we behave and whether we survive or not and yet does nothing to help us? You'll see what it does to people soon enough."

"Who is watching us?"

She stares at me without an answer.

I take a step closer. "And why are they watching?"

She holds her ground for a moment, then turns and walks away, saying nothing more.

Sixteen

Early one morning a few days later, she gives me my knife back and leads me up the cliffs with a rope ladder. She teaches me how to enter and exit the cliffs. I do better. The hardest part is the last climb from the alcove where I'd nearly died. But a noteworthy thing is happening to my mind. I feel safe around her. Confident. Her knowledge and experience is affecting me.

"Not bad," she says after I pull myself up the last wall. She grabs my hand and helps me over the final pitch.

"Thanks." I am out of breath. I bend over with my hands on my knees. Sweat drips from my forehead.

"Maybe you won't kill yourself in the first week after all."

It's a backhanded compliment but likely the best I'll get. Using the bottom of my dirty shirt, I lift it to my forehead to wick away some of the moisture. When I lower the shirt, I notice Aleah's eyes on my chest. Her eyes dart away so fast that I'm almost sure I imagined it.

"This way," she says and starts walking.

She leads me over arid hills that give onto the eastern half of the island in the low slant of the sun's early rays. Everything is golden. Shadows stretch like lines off the hills over the valleys as the sun begins to climb. Despite all the beauty on the horizon, my focus remains on her. Her strength. Her drive. It's kept her alive. Watching her overlook her island, it's almost as if she is the ruler. The Queen. *My Queen.*

As soon as the thought comes into my head, I shake it away.

Away from the roar of the surf, I hear roosters crowing in the valley below. Roosters certainly meant there were people nearby, didn't it? I am about to ask Aleah this when she suddenly freezes. She waves slowly for me to kneel behind a rock, and she hides beside me. I scan the valley below.

I hear wailing and my blood runs cold. It's the sound of agony. My eyes search for where the noise is coming from only to discover something unfathomable.

Three men hold a young woman to the ground as another group of three men with belts and ropes take turns beating a young man.

I look at Aleah. Pleading with my eyes, asking what we should do. She says nothing.

"We have to help them," I whisper, hoping my voice won't carry.

"Don't even think about it."

The young man is limp on the ground, pleading for his life as two of the men pin his arms and legs.

"They're going to kill him!"

She glares at me to watch my volume. "Yes. They are."

"Then we have to do something." Why would she just sit here and let this brutality happen? Does she have no humanity?

"Why?" she hisses. "Why do we need to help him? Do you know him? Does he mean something to you?"

"That's not the point. What they are doing. It's cruel. They're making that girl watch."

"Yes. And if you want to live, you won't interfere."

I blink at the coldness of her expression. She really is okay with letting this brutality happen. Well, I'm not. I have to do something. Anything besides allowing someone to be murdered in front of me. I rise up from my hiding spot.

She grasps at my leg and swears, but I ignore her protests and walk down the hillside toward the group. As I make my approach, I look around for anything I might use as a weapon. A stick, a rock.

Anything. I spot a good-sized rock to my left and scoop it up. I grab another the size of a ripe grapefruit. As I go, I call out to them from a distance, and they all turn and look at me.

The men glance from one to the other, and for the moment, they stop their assault on the poor man. The young woman's face is caked with tears and dirt. The man whimpers at her feet as his attackers take a few steps toward me.

"It takes six of you to hold her down and beat him?" I ask.

"What business is it of yours?" a man with a whip replies. Clearly, he's the leader of this gang. I swallow my fear. The rocks in my hands suddenly feel foolish.

I nod toward the man on the ground. "You all need to step away from him."

"Is that a fact?" The one with the whip approaches me. The whip dangles from his hand. Leather. Frayed at the end in strips.

The men are all darkly tanned. Bearded. Filthy. And every single eye is on me.

"You understand you're dead," the leader says. He snaps the whip against the ground, and the dust dances around his ankles.

Grinding my teeth, I grip my rocks tightly. "So be it."

Just then, one of the men hovering around the beaten man falls to the ground. The others turn to see what happened, when another of the men screams, clutching his arm. Through the dust I can see the young man's teeth are lodged deep into the brute's arm. Then he lets go, twists away, and takes off running.

One from the other group tries to grab him, but the young man is too quick. The others look as if they are going to give chase.

"Let him go," the leader says. "We'll find him later."

The water babbles over the rocks in the stream below, and the wind rustles the leaves of trees along the bank.

"You are going to pay," the leader says.

I process each of the men, their body language, who is most scared, who will strike first, their size, weight, height. Their stare or aversion. All of it an equation balancing in my mind as in the distance the beaten young man vanishes into the woods along the creek.

I rotate the rock loosely in my palm and draw near the leader. The leader's eyes are dark brown and bloodshot. A scar runs over his right cheek, near his ear, extending from temple to jawline.

His teeth look craggy with flesh and decay.

My focus returns to the leader's bloodshot eyes.

Hold there a moment.

Center.

The speed and precision with which I throw the rock surprises them all. It surprises me.

The sound is like a knock on a hollow piece of wood.

Pock.

The whip falls from his hand, and he crumples to the ground in a heap, landing awkwardly on his arm. He doesn't move.

The other two men step backward.

I shift the second rock from my left to my right hand and feel its gravity.

The one with the length of rope charges me, and I throw the second rock with precision and speed and strike the man between the eyes as I did with the first.

The rope falls to the ground alongside him, a small poof of dust rising as his body hits the dirt.

The third man carrying a whip looks from his two fallen brothers to the three men still holding the young woman down.

One of the three says, "Get him."

He is smaller than the two who now lie motionless on the ground. Fear in his eyes.

I bend to retrieve one of the rocks. The one with the whip swings at me. I take some of the whip on my forearm, but in doing so, I also grab the frayed ends and yank the man toward me. I swing the rock into the side of his head.

He staggers sideways and collapses. Bending down, I grab the bloodied rocks. "Who's next?"

They rise slowly from the young woman, staring at me and glancing at the three men motionless on the ground.

First one and then the other two turn and run.

The young woman watches them race away.

The leader's leg starts to stir.

A look of terror enters the young woman's eyes as she stares at me. She gets to her feet and splashes down into the creek and across the water to the bank on the other side.

"Wait!" I call out to her.

She stops, and I see a complicated mix of terror and dismay in her eyes. She holds my gaze only a moment and then turns and runs.

"Wait!" I call out again. She vanishes into the woods.

Letting out a breath, I sink to my knees and drop my weapon. My hands are covered in blood. What have I done? How did I know how to do that?

A moment later Aleah enters the clearing. She swears at me. "You are a fool," she says.

She approaches the men on the ground. I watch as without hesitation she drives her spear into his chest.

"Aleah! What are you doing?"

Instead of answering me, she repeats her action with the second man, as though it is something she's done countless times before. I see no hesitancy, aside from the breath she takes. She continues onto the third, who appears dead already from the blow to the head.

"What the hell, Aleah? You didn't have to kill them!"

She kneels beside the body and uses the man's shirt to wipe her spear clean.

"You have no idea what you just did."

"What *I* did? I didn't kill them! I just stopped them from hurting that man."

"And by doing so, signed your own death sentence. Those men you left alive? They will hunt you down for what you've done here today. And if they hunt you, then they hunt me, too."

She glares at me. She drops down into the creek, rinses her hands, and then fills her leather bota, looking for any sign of the others as she does so.

She drinks.

Then she climbs the bank and looks at me once again.

She wipes water from her chin. I stare at her as she starts to walk away.

Seventeen

I look at her at the mouth of the cave, certain she wants to push me off the cliff.

"I don't know what to say." She shakes her head, a frown of disgust on her lips.

"I should've what, stood there and watched them kill him in front of her?"

"It's done. You did what you did. Now you have to live with the consequences. And I have to live with it because I took you in."

"I couldn't just watch that happen and do nothing."

"You don't understand a thing about this island, yet you rush in like that." She says, "Those three that got away—"

"They would've killed him. What would they have done to her? Use your imagination."

"I don't have to use my imagination," she says. "I've seen what they'll do firsthand."

"I know what's right."

"You know what's right?" She laughs. It's high-pitched as if she's on the verge of losing control. "You?"

She swears several times.

"This is sick," she says. She turns to face the ocean. "I can't do it. I cannot do it."

"What is the matter with you?"

She turns on me, and I see something flash in her eyes. She hitches her thumb at herself. "What is the matter with *me*?"

Before I can react, she grabs her spear and pushes me against the wall. She puts the point to my throat and stands looking into my eyes.

"You have the gall to ask me what is the matter with *me?*" Her voice is low, menacing.

"I did the right thing thing."

"There is no right. That world doesn't exist anymore. Right or wrong. They don't exist here. This island doesn't know right or wrong. It knows survival."

"You would've done the same thing. You would've saved him. I see the good in you, Aleah. And I see what this world has done to you."

She turns, pulls the spear away from my throat, and points to the mouth of the cave. "You need to go."

"What?"

"Leave," she says. "Leave now! Get out of my sight. I never want to see you again." Her last words are so quiet I barely catch them.

For a moment, I stand there in disbelief. When it becomes clear she isn't taking back her demand, anger rises inside of my chest like a thunderhead. "Where am I supposed to go?"

She turns her back to me and whispers, "Anywhere but here."

Eighteen

I stand on the edge and look down at the cliffs below. Of course, I'll honor her demand. I'll not violate her trust again, but I don't understand why she killed those men. I don't understand the intensity of her reaction to me, and I don't understand this island. I stumble up the hill a bit to where I can see the ocean in every direction. Were I not overwhelmed with such doubt and confusion, I'm sure I'd think the expanse of the blue beautiful, glimmering as it is in the sunlight. But all I know is that I'm lost and alone.

But I'm fearful now of returning to the creek, as the men I let get away may return in greater numbers looking to kill me. And, I now realize, to kill Aleah because of my actions.

Despair squeezes my heart like a clenched fist, and I nearly choke on it. How much more can I endure? Why am I here? What can't I remember? And what is really going on?

I think of the boy who died in my arms and begin walking down toward the beach. I know it'll take a few hours, but nothing else makes sense, so why not go back to the beginning? Besides, leaving the boy, the raft, and briefcase seems rash. Perhaps there are clues I overlooked. Maybe I can figure out how to open the thing now.

I pass a tree with a camera high up in its branches. It looks as though someone has marked the tree with blood or clay, a red mixture that forms a large "X." I pause for a moment looking up at it.

X

When I finally reach the beach and the turquoise water of the lagoon, I see the destroyed raft and the shine of the chrome metal briefcase, but the boy's body is gone from its sandy grave. The palm fronds that I used to cover it are askew and hoofprints, hundreds of them, surround the grave. With a sickening realization, I see the drag marks leading toward the swampy mangrove swamp.

Whatever took his body, likely wild pigs, had not cared about the briefcase or the raft.

I follow the drag marks until they vanish into the briny water of the mangrove swamp. I stand at the edge, my ankles and shoes covered in mud and sand. Mosquitoes swarm as I pull back branches and peer into the murky depths. But the body is nowhere to be found.

Back at the beach, I drop down at the water's edge and take off my shoes and socks to dig my toes into the sand. I pull off my shirt and swish it in the water in a feeble attempt to clean it. Then I lay it out on the sand out of reach of the surf and rest my elbows on my knees. The water laps at the shoreline of the lagoon as the sun dips below the ocean's horizon, and I wonder if anyone is watching me from the high rocky cliffs at either end of the beach.

Nineteen

I lean back, rest my head on my drying shirt, and let my mind drift. I gaze up at the stars and listen to the waves break on the reef. What if I build a raft out of wood gathered from the mangrove swamp? I swat away flying insects from my face. What if I can get away and discover what all this is about? I'd come back. I wouldn't leave these people here, forgotten. Forgetting.

A twig snaps in the swampy darkness behind me. I roll over and scan the woods but can see nothing. I pull my knife from my pocket and flick it open as I rise to my knees, trying to keep my body low. Something is moving under the trees. Someone.

I see their contours in the dappled moonlight filtering to the ground through the treetops. My heart beats fast in my chest. My fingers tighten around the knife handle.

"Jordan," she calls from the darkness.

"Aleah?"

She emerges from the darkness at the sound of my voice and lowers her spear. I rise to my feet and watch as she approaches.

"I thought I might find you here."

"What're you doing?"

"I made a mistake."

I stare at her in the moonlight, the lean angular features of her face, her piercing eyes. She jams her spear down into the sand like a staff, the tip pointed to the sky. She looks at my bare feet, then up into my eyes.

"It was not easy for me to come here to say this."

Sensing the turmoil inside her, I want to fill the silence and tell her that it's okay, that she doesn't need to struggle to find the right words, that I accept her as she is.

"It's enough," I say. "You are enough."

She stares up at me, and for a second it looks as if she might cry. I move toward her and take her in my arms, feel her breath catch in her chest.

"Just as you are," I whisper into her hair.

How long has she been here? How long has she been alone? How many times has she had to kill to stay alive? I can't know everything's she's been through, and I can't understand all the pain, but instinctively I want to ease her suffering.

"I'm here," I whisper. "I care."

Her arms wrap around me, pulling me closer. I feel the rise and fall of her chest. Her body is warm against mine. After a moment, she pushes away from me, wipes her tears with a knuckle, and turns to gaze out at the moonlight glimmering on the sea.

"I used to think this place was an experiment," she says. "They clear each new arrival of memories and drop us here to see if we can survive the ocean, how we'll organize, who we'll love or kill, and if you're able to find your way toward peace and understanding. Of your true self. Of humanity, maybe."

"What do you think now?"

"I don't think it's an experiment at all. I think this island is real life, a reflection of our world, our inability to know our past lives, or what, if anything, lies after this life. It's a reflection of every human being's hopes and dreams that there's more to this existence."

"And what's the matter with that?" I ask, pushing a strand of hair away from her tear-streaked face.

She looks over at the items on the beach, kneels and picks up the briefcase, runs her fingers over the latches. She lifts the destroyed raft and sees the life vest with the markings on the lapel.

Her gaze shoots toward me.

"That could be useful, yes?"

She draws in a long breath. "What if everything you thought was reality was a lie?"

"You're talking about the cameras," I say. "The watchers."

She puts the life vest beside the chrome metal briefcase. "Was there anything else in the raft?"

"The canteen. The knife."

"That's it?"

"That's it. Besides the cameras." I look toward the boy's grave. "Something took the boy's body. There are hoofprints leading to the swamp."

I show her where I buried him. She stares down at the shallow grave for a long time.

"Why are we aware of our own mortality?" Her voice sounds almost distracted, dreamlike.

"Why are we here, Aleah?" I ask, stepping closer to her. "Who put us here?"

"We are here to survive," she says.

"Is that all there is to a meaningful life?"

"What was he like?"

"The boy?"

She nods.

"He was scared," I say. "He tried to kill me during our first night at sea. Tried to stab me with that knife. Something was wrong with him."

"Wrong with him?"

"Like they'd scrambled his brain. He couldn't look at me, and he talked out loud to himself. He was full of facts and arcane information. Obviously smart. Maybe brilliant."

"You cared for him?"

"He was alone." I shrug, unable—or unwilling—to articulate what I feel.

"If we know that people came before us, and we know we're going to die," she says, "the whole reason we've developed this awareness of our mortality is so that we work to leave the world a better place for our children, for all the others who will live after us. That awareness would emerge through natural selection."

"You want a rational explanation for the purpose of life and yet you killed those men without hesitation?"

"Men are a cancer—"

"Those men," I clarify.

"I've yet to be persuaded otherwise."

"We choose to see things how we want to see them." It sounds trite, but I know it's true.

"Like heartache."

"Heartache, suffering," I say. "They're all perceptions. We choose how we perceive, how we feel about a situation, others, about ourselves."

"I just need to know that I can trust you, Jordan."

"You never tried to leave?"

"Are you listening to me?"

"You said you need to know you can trust me."

"And I need you to trust me." She touches my arm. "No matter what."

"No matter what," I say.

She takes in a deep breath and lets it out slowly. "So, get this straight. You can't leave the island."

I watch her as her mind drifts into memory. Something troubles her. Her brow furrows, the corners of her mouth dip down in a frown.

"What happened to you?" I ask. I know the trauma she's experienced is bone-deep.

"Everyone I've ever gotten close to on this island has either been killed or has turned against me."

"That's why you're alone?"

"I can't let anyone in."

We stare at one another. Suddenly she moves forward, and she presses her lips against mine. Through the thin fabric of her shirt on my bare chest, her breasts are warm, inviting. Her hand moves to my face, cradling my jaw, then down my arms to my waist.

"I want you to let me in," I say.

"I don't know if I can do this." She unfastens my pants and pushes them down over my hips. I suck in a breath as she takes hold of me.

I begin to lift her shirt, hesitating, but she doesn't resist. Instead, she raises her arms and I pull it off over her head.

"But I want you," she says, her hand drifting back down my chest, my abdomen, lower. "I want you inside me."

I kick off my pants and pull hers off and we're both naked, standing at the water's edge. The moonlight glimmers like diamonds, and she sinks to her knees, trailing her fingers along my thighs, then pulling me down with her. She climbs over me, straddles me, sinking down and guiding me into her. Her hips move up and down, and I meet her every movement as she moans in pleasure, saying yes, yes, yes. I stare up at her in awe as she steadies herself with hands on my chest and throws her head back and looks up at the stars in the night sky.

"I've wanted this for so long," she says. "You have no idea how long."

"Yes." It seems to be all I can say.

"Faster, Jordan," she cries out.

"Yes."

"Faster. Harder."

"Yes," I gasp.

"As if our lives depend on it."

And, instinctively, I know they do.

PART 2

Twenty

The boat is in distress.

Days after reconciling with Aleah, I spot it out on the water a good mile or more from the island. I alert her. As we stand at the mouth of the cave, I watch her reaction.

"Others will see it," she says.

"How can you be sure?"

The boat is without a sail. It floats on the surface as though it has taken on water. Sluggish on the waves, it tips back and forth.

I squint into the distance. "Do you see anyone? It looks abandoned."

"This is trouble," she says.

"What do we do?"

She takes a deep breath and sighs. Her eyes narrow. "We should follow it," she says. "There might be supplies."

"Supplies?" I say. "It might be our way off this island."

"You know how to sail?"

"I don't remember." I quirk a smile at her. "But I want to say yes."

"Jordan, all that boat is good for is whatever supplies are on it."

"Why is that?"

"Because you can't leave the island. They'll not let you."

"Who? Who is 'they'?"

"The watchers." She retrieves her spear. Throws the life vest at me to bring. "You're going to get me killed. Mark my words."

Twenty-one

We come down off a hill onto part of the island that I've not yet seen. A sandy peninsula gives way to a rocky shoreline that juts out into the water near the mouth of the channel.

"Once you get out there," she cautions, "the current is strong."

"You're coming, too?"

"Of course."

I can't tell exactly how far the smaller island extends on the opposite side, but it looks as though the boat might hit it.

"What's it like on the other side?"

"The waves come in hard. There's no reef protecting it."

"You wear the vest." I hold it out to her.

She looks at me. "You're sure?"

"We'll stay together." I know it's the right decision, but anxiety gnaws at me as we wade out over the rocks and into the deeper water.

She swears and shoots a look my way. Is she afraid? Angry? I can't tell.

"Here," I say. "Hold onto me."

We continue out into the channel.

"Know the depth?" I look down. The water is clear, but I can't see the bottom.

"Pretty deep. I rarely swim out here."

"Great."

We swim farther out.

"You want to switch?" She must sense my anxiety. "I can swim without it."

I swear and shake my head. "No, I'm okay. I just don't want to be half-eaten by a shark." Like the boy. I push the image of his mangled, bloodied body away, take a deep breath, and keep going.

When we reach the beach of the smaller island, I stand in my soaked clothes and look out at the boat bobbing and weaving toward us from the open sea.

"What do you think?" She takes a drink from her leather bota as I sip from my canteen. She removes cooked meat from her pocket and eats. She hands a strip to me. I wave it off. My arms feel heavy. I don't want to admit it, but the thought of eating right now makes me queasy.

"You did alright."

"We made it," I say.

Twenty-two

I follow her up a hill until we reach a ridge that opens onto a northwestern view. The drifting sailboat comes toward us. It will make landfall right below us. An involuntary shiver makes me laugh. "This whole thing makes me nervous."

"It should."

Down below, the ocean beats against the side of the island. The shoreline is steep and rocky, and the waves hit the cliffs in huge swells that send ocean spray up into the air.

"A fall out here," I say, "and it's all over."

"I don't even know if I could put it into words."

I turn to her. "What?"

"How difficult this is for me."

"You think this is a mistake? That we should turn back?" My wet clothes cling to my skin. My waterlogged shoes are heavy on my feet, making me feel clumsy.

"There's a ledge." She points. "How do you feel about—"

"Jumping?"

She nods.

"Not great. But I can do it." I study her face, which is tight with worry. "You're filling me with confidence."

"Don't be funny," she says. "Not about this."

"What?"

She draws in a long breath and gives her head a little shake. "Stay here. I'll go. I'll swim for it."

"How're you supposed to get back up?"

She points to a spot far in the distance where the cliff slopes down to the sea. Her hand is shaking.

"No." I hold out my hand. "Give me the life vest. I'll do it."

"Stop it." She steps back. "Please don't."

I try to take it from her, but she refuses.

"Give it to me. Aleah, please."

Her eyes hold a terror I don't understand.

"I need to do this," I say. "Hey, look at me. It's okay."

Her expression is flat. "Yeah."

"Everything's going to be alright."

"Of course." Now her voice is flat.

Still, I take the vest and put it on, then clamber down the hill to the ledge below and stop, gazing down into the water. It looks deep.

The boat is closer. Forty feet from stern to bow, it rides low and heavy on the swells.

I look up at her. Even from here, I can tell she's worried.

I shake my head, give her a thumbs up. Then I turn and run toward the ledge, leaping out into the air.

Twenty-three

Even with the life vest on, the weight of my body drags me deep into the blue, and I don't hold my breath right on the way down.

Panic.

I rise to the surface quickly and am struck by a huge wave, twisted around, and see the rocks of the cliff coming at me. I swing around and pump my arms, trying to swim out and away from danger. My body is pushed up on a huge swell, slides down the back. Rising higher, plunging deeper. The waves explode against the cliffs. I force my arms to churn, my legs to kick.

The waves come at me, battering, deafening.

One after another.

I swim. Arms cutting through the waves. Feet pushing off rocks, legs kicking. Blood pumping. Adrenaline surging.

Harder.

Can't breathe.

My heart feels like it might explode.

Another wave.

I rise up on the crest, almost at the point of a breaker, slide down the back and continue out away from the island.

To calmer water.

I approach the boat. The hull is painted pale blue like the sky. The mast is broken. At one point it might have had a roller-furling jib, but all that remains is a broken rusted cable and a tattered shred of cloth draping out in the water like a manta.

Something in my brain remembers boats. I'm not sure why or how, but nautical terms come to me, and I understand them, terms that are surely not common knowledge.

Wires and ropes wrap around the decks.

I swim toward the stern.

Half of the rudder is all that remains, and it swings out like a broken limb.

A swim ladder clings to the back.

I climb it and immediately see water sloshing around inside the dark salon in front of me.

I look back to shore and see Aleah on the cliff. I wave to indicate I am okay. She does not return the gesture. I can see her arms clamped around her body.

I climb down onto the rear hull deck and try the wheel. It rotates a few inches, then jams. The remains of the rudder swing back and forth only a bit.

I walk forward to the companionway above the salon.

Steps lead down into the darkness. Water fills the cabin floor, and debris floats in the murk.

I reason through the boat's path on the current and wind. A steady, low-level release of adrenaline makes it difficult to breathe or think calmly. My hands tremble. I force myself to take deep breaths, calm my nerves.

The boat rocks on the huge swells. It will be battered against the rocks soon, and it isn't navigable in its current state. Maybe I can try to lay anchor, stop it from crashing into the cliffs. Heading forward to the port side, careful to step over the cables and lines strewn in disarray, I try to stay low so as not to lose balance on the waves.

I find a forward locker, open it, and see a large anchor inside, chains, and a huge pile of rope. I look down into the water over the side. The anchor will do no good if it's too deep, even with all the rope.

Short of throwing it over, I have no way to gauge depth.

Nonetheless it's the one option that may save the boat from the rocks, provided the anchor can reach the bottom. I return to the steps down into the salon and interior of the boat.

Twenty-four

The water comes up to my waist as I stand in the interior. A soggy box of snack food brushes against my side. I pick it up and look closely.

My finger traces the shapes "o," "n," and "r" on the box and then rises to the similar markings on my life vest.

A seat cushion floats ahead of me.

Looking forward, I see a narrow hallway. Everything below the deck is filled with water. I wade toward the hall and forward berths.

A red, plastic first-aid kit floats. I pluck it out of the water and open it. Gauze, tape, ointment. Maybe useful. The kit is watertight. I close it, toss it back toward the steps to the hull.

Small bathroom on the left. A narrow cabin on the right. A larger cabin forward.

All of it submerged.

Without a working bilge, it would take days to bucket the level down to the floor. Even still, hundreds of gallons would remain in the bottom of the hull beneath the cabin floor.

A book floating in the water catches my attention. I pick it up and study the letters on the front. *Al Noroeste del Caribe*. I turn the waterlogged pages carefully and see that the book is filled with thousands of—

"Words," I say aloud.

Only then does it finally sink in that these markings—these words—are clues all around me. I recall the conversation with the kid on the raft about the markings on my life vest, but the importance of words had not really sunk in at the time because there were only the letters on my vest and on the raft.

But now, surrounded in this vessel by so many words, I wonder what they all mean and suspect they could help me understand this place or even who I am. Somehow, I know I used to understand them. I used to be able to...*what?*

I look at the markings on my life jacket again:

JOR. V. 3.2

ANAG. NORISIS, INC.

"I don't know how to make meaning from these things," I say aloud. "Letters and words."

I carry the book and the first-aid kit up onto the deck and place them on a seat by the wheel.

I look back at the island and do not see Aleah. I freeze. Scan the cliffs. She's gone.

I'll worry more about that later. For now, I am going to have to use the anchor. There's no way around it. Either it will or it won't hold, but I only have minutes before the boat will reach the cliffs.

I lean over the stern and see words like the one on my life jacket and like the ones in the waterlogged book and on the boxes inside the vessel. I'd not noticed them when I'd climbed aboard the first time, but I'm putting it together now that these markings on the boat are letters that form words that I cannot read but that would likely help me to make sense of who I am, where I am, and why I am here.

Marina Del Rey, CA

Anag. Norisis, Inc.

And then it hits me: I don't know how to read. The realization fills me with wonder and frustration. And then shame. Shame because I feel inept that I don't know how to make meaning from the words painted on the back of the boat. Shame because I'm surrounded by clues that I cannot decipher.

Twenty-five

I open the locker, lift the anchor, and begin to feed it over the bow. I watch it descend into the clear blue. The rope slides through my hands.

I am paying out a lot. Nearly half the line is down when I feel the weight come to rest on the bottom.

Then I continue to feed more rope as the boat drifts closer to the cliffs. The line stretches out at an angle, and the boat slowly starts to turn so that the bow is pointed toward the anchor. When I'm done I've used nearly all of the rope, but the boat seems to hold its position. Still, it makes me nervous.

I secure the line to the bow cleat and realize I know how to do all this. Then I stand there and study whether I'm drifting anymore.

Don't seem to be.

The coastline along this side of the small island looks like one jagged wall of rock. The only break in the formation appears down island where the ridge descends out into the water. At this distance however, I can't tell for sure whether there is a feasible path from the ocean onto the lower steps of the ridge.

I'm exhausted. My arms, back, and shoulders ache. And I don't know where Aleah is.

•••

Below deck again, I wade through the water. I search cabinets and lockers submerged beneath the surface. I find pots and pans and cooking supplies. On one bottle I see a picture of an olive and inside the bottle a viscous clear liquid. I find a can with a picture of a split coconut and another with pictures of beans.

"They erased my ability to read," I say aloud, still stunned by the idea, baffled by why anyone would want to do such a thing to another person. Then I continue to work. I search more drawers and cabinets. Find a fire extinguisher, forks, and knives. I add them to the pile.

Linens and towels soaked and folded. Clothes. Jeans. Shorts. A pair of sneakers. A hat. Sunglasses.

I find a pair of binoculars on the bulkhead.

Water has gotten behind the lenses. I can hear it sloshing around inside, but I might be able to salvage them.

I go above deck and try using them. Adjust the focus. No use. Perhaps I could disassemble it and clean them out later.

I add them to my pile and then scrutinize the cliffs.

Still no Aleah.

•••

I inspect the anchor line. The white rope descends over the side, taut and straight down into the clear blue ocean. The boat rises and falls on the swells. I center myself and stay low to keep my balance.

I inspect the jib cables strewn out in the water on the port side. The tattered remains of the sail float on the blue. I haul it in. Water pours from the fabric as I pull it up from the ocean and onto the boat.

All the while, I keep watch along the cliffs for Aleah.

I slide the sail free of the jib and bundle it all up in my arms. I carry it toward the wheel, where I lay it out to dry.

My eyes catch the shine of metal latches on the benches by the wheel. I open one.

Life jackets, ropes, and rolls of fabric beneath.

I remove the jackets and ropes and place them in the hutch by the companion steps with the pile of supplies from below deck. I inspect the rolled and folded fabric.

Spare sails.

I stare at them, let that sink in a moment.

Then I take another long scan of the cliffs.

My pulse quickens. I sweat under the blazing sun.

•••

From one of the bedding sheets, I make a bindle. I place the supplies I've gathered so far in it and tie it up and fasten it to one of the life jackets.

Something catches my eye.

I scan the tanned rocky cliffs and see her on a distant ridge down island.

She looks tiny. The sun scorches the ocean and earth. I cup my hand over my eyes to shield them from the glare. She waves her arms over her head.

I return the wave. She walks down the ridge toward the ocean.

I tighten the straps of my life vest and then carry my bindle of supplies tied to two life jackets buckled together. I throw the bindle, leap out into the ocean beside it, and begin to swim.

Twenty-six

"You don't know how to read either," I say to her.

"What?"

I spread out the supplies on the dry earth to show her. I point to the letters and words, pick up the book.

"I know the objects," I say. "Book, can, beans, olives. But the words on the front—inside here—I don't know what they mean. They removed my ability to read words and numbers."

"Why would someone do that?"

"When were you going to tell me?" I ask.

She freezes. "Tell you what?"

"About things like this." I hold the book.

"Who cares if you know how to read or not?" she says. "Who cares if you know numbers? All that matters is survival."

"Aleah, if we knew how to read, these things would tell us where we are, who we are, maybe even why we're here."

"None of which matters for surviving today. Today is what matters. *Survival* is what matters."

I look into her eyes. "I know the words on the back of that boat say where it's from, but I can't read them. Whoever put us here erased our ability to read words and numbers because they don't want us to decode the clues all around us. They don't want us to get off this island."

I study her face. She holds my gaze.

"You can't leave," she whispers.

"Why not? I'd like to know where I am. And *when* I am. And why we're here. Where that boat is from. *Who I am!*"

"You're losing it."

"Is this how you establish trust? By keeping secrets?" I try to calm myself, modulate my voice, and sound reasonable. "At least you have a name."

"I made my name up," she says. "I don't really know who I am or why I'm here. No living creature can know that. Anywhere. Anytime. What matters to me is that I have food to eat tonight, a place to sleep. You're wasting energy trying to figure out who put us here or why they did it."

"How can you not want to know who you are?"

"Maybe I know who I am just fine, and I can't stand it." She closes her eyes, drags her hand through her hair. "Maybe I'd rather not know who I was in the past or what I've done. Maybe it'd be nice if I could just live in the present and not think about what happened then or torment myself about where I am now or where I think I need to be when I have everything I need right here."

"You can't go anywhere until you know where you are."

"Dammit, I don't want to go anywhere!" Her voice is tinged with desperation. "Can't you get that through your head? There's nothing out there worth seeing!"

"There are extra sails on that boat."

This stops her for a moment. Then she shakes her head. "You're a fool if you keep pursuing this," she says. "That boat is nothing but trouble. People will kill one another over it. The best we can hope for is the supplies you've collected. You did good, Jordan. Now we need to stay alive."

•••

We camp down on the beach after nightfall. Hungry. Exhausted. Nearly out of fresh water.

Neither sleeps much.

I keep a watchful eye on the starlit channel.

At some point in the middle of the night, Aleah rises and walks down to the water. She clips on the extra life jacket I brought from the boat and picks up the bindle tied to the spare life jacket.

"We might as well swim back," she says.

"I don't like the idea of swimming at night."

She looks up at the ridge line. "Safer under cover of night in case others saw the boat and come to find it."

Twenty-seven

Under cover of darkness, we reach a sandy beach on the big island. The cool water sloughs off me as I stand. Aleah touches my shoulder and raises a finger to her lips.

I look at her in the moonlight standing in the water with her life jacket buckled, her hair slicked back and wet from the swim, the spear held in her right hand.

Motionless.

She scans the palm trees beyond the beach.

I see nothing but darkness. Branches rustle and sway in a breeze coming down from the hillside and out over the channel behind us.

I whisper, "See anything?"

Her eyes fix on the shadows within the trees beyond the beach. She raises her finger to her lips, motions for me to hand her the bindle.

I do so. She carries it up onto the beach.

I flick open my knife and follow her, flanking her as she goes.

She drops to one knee and motions for me to do the same. She raises the spear and points it up toward the trees. Slowly she sweeps the tip along the treeline searching for movement.

I hear only the sound of the surf on the beach, the breeze rustling palm fronds, my own breathing, Aleah's exhalations just a few feet from me, water from our bodies dripping on the sand.

Suddenly a whistling sound comes from the sky. I look up. See a light falling toward us.

Aleah swears.

The object's whistle becomes a high-pitched whine as it falls to the earth. It crashes on the beach, not more than thirty feet from us.

Cautiously, we approach and see that the object is roughly the size of a storage trunk. It's made of black carbon fiber, and it has hit the sand at the wrong angle. We walk around it and see that the impact side is dented. There are four rotor blades, one at each corner, and red lights flicker along the sides of its body.

Two of the rotor blades are damaged, broken and bent, and only one of the other two is spinning. The motors sound like wounded animals, struggling to stay alive.

I see more unintelligible words printed on the side of the unit in red: EDEN 2.

"What in the world?" I whisper.

"Stay back," she says, whipping her arm back across my abdomen to keep me from getting closer.

On the sides of its body, small slats open, and mechanical legs try to emerge. Only one extends its full length and is able to bend to touch the sand. Three other arms keep extending partially and then retracting as though some internal mechanism is broken and does not allow them to fully reach the ground.

The one functional leg claws at the sand and tries to raise the whole unit up by itself.

I just stare.

On the bottom of the unit what appears to be a tubular camera lens pivots in the sand, its lens likely shattered and buried a few inches underground. Rotating disks turn back and forth as though trying to focus the buried lens. It makes a whirring noise as it clicks back and forth.

"Bird." I say, pointing to feathers lodged in the casing of one of the rotors and blood smears along the top of the unit. "See? Part of a wing is lodged in one of the damaged rotor blades. What do you make of it?"

"Some kind of drone."

I crouch near the side of the unit by the leg that continues to paw ineffectively at the sand. As I approach, the mechanical extension stops moving. Digital lights on the unit flicker, and a small camera lens on the side rotates and points at me.

It focuses, as though sensing my presence.

I hold my knife in hand.

"Don't get too close," Aleah hisses.

The leg stops pawing at the sand and shoots out toward me. Its tip curls like a prehensile tail trying to grab me, but I quickly retreat beyond its reach, stumbling backward and landing on my backside.

I swear, and Aleah helps me to my feet. She spots something on the ground at the top of the beach, walks there, and retrieves it. A heavy stone the size of a coconut.

She hands me the spear and then approaches the limb, which swings around in the air like a tentacle.

She stands just out of reach as it extends fully to try to get at her. Then, it seems to sense she is beyond its reach, drops back to the sand, and tries to raise its body again. The other limbs wave wildly, trying to extend without success.

Aleah raises the stone above her head and then swings down hard, striking the one good limb. Sparks explode from inside the unit.

She steps back.

She's broken a pin in one of its joints. It still tries to claw at the sand and air, but its range of motion is now limited.

She watches it a moment more, then steps forward briskly and swings down harder with the stone and breaks the mechanical limb off completely. It falls to the sand and ceases moving.

She studies it.

Lifeless.

She picks it up.

The length of a human arm, the piece is narrow and consists of interlocking carbon fiber joints that enable it to bend and move and twist.

I manage to turn the body of the unit over. It is surprisingly light. The large telescopic camera lens on its underside is shattered.

"We could carry this."

"We're not carrying that thing anywhere."

"What the hell is it?"

"They're always watching us," she says. "I told you that."

She takes the stone and begins battering the body. She crushes any visible camera lens and keeps smashing, bringing the stone down on the black box over and over again.

"I think it's dead, Aleah."

She says nothing. Instead, she carries it to the edge of the water, retrieves the stone, and bashes the unit a dozen times more. Then she picks it up and flings it out to sea. In the moonlight, I watch as it seems to sit on the surface for a moment and then sinks into the depths.

"Everything we say and do is observed," she says. "Get that through your head. And if I say the wrong thing, I'll be dead in a matter of hours."

I stare at her.

"All of this—" She motions to the beach and island and ocean. "—is a constructed reality. Nothing is real."

"Nothing?"

"Nothing."

"But you're real."

"Jordan, nothing," she says, holding my gaze, "*nothing* is real."

Twenty-eight

When we enter the cave, the chrome suitcase is open. The base appears to be a keyboard but also contains inset dials and blinking green, yellow, and red digital lights. The vertical part of the interior of the case is a screen. On it, a woman's image is frozen.

"Do you recognize her?" I ask.

Aleah says nothing.

The woman is dressed in a blue and white form-fitting jacket with a zipper on the front. Her hair is shaved short, and her eyes are like a forest, shades of dark green and brown. Her jawline tapers heart-like to a strong round chin. Her lips are closed, and her left ear is pierced with a small round blue stone.

Her face is a contrast of fierce and beautiful, rugged and serene. The shaved hair and toughness of her facial features give her an almost military edge, but her eyes blue as the ocean suggest wisdom that comes from compassion and a lifetime of facing irreconcilable choices.

The image on the screen comes to life and begins speaking.

"I don't have much time. They're coming for us. My name is Perí Peteia. Dr. Perí Peteia. And I can only hope that if you've found this, you're alive and that it hasn't fallen into the wrong hands. Your name is Jordan. Remember that."

She pauses for a second, trying to find her words. It seems as though this last statement has struck an emotional nerve inside her. She takes a deep breath and exhales.

Suddenly the sound of a young girl off-camera rings out, a sort of feral shriek.

The woman turns toward the girl, and banging sounds erupt as if someone is trying to beat down a door. The woman reaches out, picks the girl up in her arms, and turns to face the camera. The girl, perhaps six or seven, looks scared. Her eyes are brown with speckles of deep blue around the edges. Her face is lean, her lips a tense flat line, and her sand-colored hair has been dyed with streaks of blue.

The woman says, "You must leave the island. We have a small force far to the north on the mainland, survivors underground in the ruins of the Anag Norisis compound. If you are able to reach us and I'm still alive, we can help you to retrieve your memories. We can help you to understand the Plague, the Fallout, and the Clear."

An explosion shakes the image on the screen, and the young girl cries out.

The woman looks back at the camera. "Everything on the island is going to change. They're going to kill you all and start anew. I was going to stop them, but I've just learned th—"

The image goes blank.

I stare at the screen for a moment in silence, waiting for it to continue.

A hissing sound comes from within the suitcase as though from hydraulics, and it begins to close. I reach forward and try to keep it open, but the mechanical force is powerful, and I withdraw my hands before they are crushed.

"There might be more," I say. "There may be other things."

I wrench at the buckles on the front, but they don't budge. The case seals shut.

"How did it open?" I say. "We need to understand why it opened." I stare at the suitcase and then turn to Aleah. "How did you know my name?"

"I've told you nothing on this island is what it seems."

"What the hell?"

"They were listening when I came up with that name."

"I had this briefcase before you called me that," I say. "And besides, you said there were no cameras here in the cave. You said you'd scoured every inch—"

"That's not what I said. I said I've scoured every square inch of the mouth of this cave but that there are probably others. I told you I choose to behave as though I'm being watched at all times."

I look into her eyes and realize I can't discern whether or not she's telling the truth.

She continues, "There's no way to know when that message was recorded or even if it's real. It could be a staged video with actors, transmitted to a receiver in this thing."

"All set up after they heard you call me 'Jordan'?"

She says, "It's the only way to explain it."

"The only way?" I ask. "She said they're going to kill us all."

"It's a setup. Why would they allow you to find this? You said it was in the raft."

"I took it with me into the raft. I found it floating beside me when I came to." I pause and consider the expression on her face. "You've never seen anything like it?"

"What do you think?" she says.

"What do you *know*, Aleah?"

She walks to the mouth of the cave, then turns around to face me. "I know that I love you. And that I learned long ago you can't accept anything on this island as truth or reality."

Twenty-nine

I can't sleep.

I lie in the darkness, mulling over the name "Jordan" and listening to the ocean and the snap and hiss of dying embers. Every once in a while, a spark shoots up toward the ceiling, and I follow them with my eyes and gaze up at the roof of the cave, wondering how long Aleah has been here, how long she's been alone. Wondering what's real and what's a lie.

I look at Aleah lying on her side, her face illuminated in the light from the fire's glow. Her eyes are open, fixed on me.

I want to know if I can believe anything she's told me.

Perhaps she wants the same thing.

We look at each other, and neither says a word.

Thirty

In the morning she asks, "How would you fix the mast?"

The question takes me by surprise. I thought she was opposed to the idea of returning to the ship.

"Why do you ask?"

"Why don't you tell me your idea?"

"We'd have to cut a tree to fit the mast boot and step it just the same as a metal mast."

"A tree?"

"There are some tall enough along the creek."

Her eyes gaze into my own. "You think it would sail?"

"If we bailed out the water and fixed the mast, probably," I say. "Hard to know how much damage is beneath the water line. But it got here. If there was a bad leak, it would've never made it this far."

We look at one another for a long time.

"What do you remember from before the island?" I ask her.

"Nothing."

"Nothing at all?"

She shakes her head. "As far as I'm concerned, that person never existed."

Thirty-one

When we reach the smaller island, the rain is coming down in drenching sheets. Aleah is first on the beach. She removes her spear from its sheath on her back and holds it in her hand, ready for whatever happens next. I stagger and fall to my knees in the wet sand.

"Are you okay?" Rain streaks down her face, hair, shoulders, arms, and chest.

"I'll be okay." My arms are numb with exhaustion from swimming across the channel.

"You sure?"

I glance up at her and nod. "I just really don't like swimming across that channel in the dark. In the rain. With the waves and not knowing what is swimming in the water beneath me."

She looks at me for a moment, then reaches out her hand for me to take. "Well, we made it."

I take her hand and rise to my feet, brushing off the sand from my tattered pants legs. "Yeah."

We set up camp on the beach in the darkness. I don't understand how she can eat. She chews the meat, drinks the water from her bota, and coughs in the driving rain.

"We should head inland," she says. "See if this storm has destroyed your boat."

I follow her up a steep hillside through seaside foliage. We enter a wooded area near a ridge high above the ocean, and I watch flashes of lightning far in the distance brighten the sky and dark ocean. Wind whips around us. Trees creak and sway in the gusting rain. Footing is slippery.

She leads me to a clearing on the opposite side of the small island. High above the ocean, I recognize the narrow slope that juts out into the sea like a terrace with sheer cliffs on three sides: left, right, and forward. It is the cliff from which I'd leapt into the sea before swimming to the boat.

The rain beats against us as we descend the trail. When we reach the end of the cliff, I spy the boat down below, anchored just as I'd left it.

Six men are on it.

They shout at one another and, in an assembly line, bucket water from down below. The boat no longer sits as low on the sea. It rocks fiercely in the storm, but the anchorage holds. They've raised a mast that sways precariously on the violent ocean.

Aleah waves me back from the end of the cliff.

It is then that I see a dozen of their kind emerge from the woods up the ridge. They're all older, bearded and filthy, emaciated and adorned with bone necklaces and animal carcasses. They're armed with handmade whips, maces, and knives, and they have us trapped on the cliff that juts out into the sea.

I recognize two of them. The ones I'd let escape.

Lightning crackles across the sky, and in the flash, I see fear in Aleah's eyes as I never have before. Another half dozen emerge behind the first twelve.

"Remember what I told you," she whispers. "Don't let them take you alive."

The men descend the trail toward us.

"Aleah," a man in front calls out.

"I have no quarrel with you, Syker."

"If you're allied with this—thing—you'll have to pay, my dear girl."

"What do you want from us?"

"He killed three. You know the penalty."

She raises her spear and unsheathes her knife.

Lightning flashes across the ocean behind her. Rain hammers down.

"Why'd you come back?" the one named Syker asks her. He wears a deer carcass, antlers rising like horns from his head. "You knew we'd be here."

"You know why I came."

"You were hoping to find me then," Syker says, with a knowing nod.

"I was here before any of you arrived and began making your 'laws'."

"The moral laws come from those who put us here."

"You have no idea who put us here, and I'll kill every last one of you if you come a step closer."

"Aleah, you're outnumbered." Syker says this almost gently.

Her eyes flick toward me then back to Syker. "So be it."

I thumb open my knife. My heart sinks as I watch the sheer number of them close off any escape from the rocky cliff toward the interior of the small island.

Aleah turns and says, "You know the spot to leap from the cliff. Run. I'll fight them off as long as I can."

"No," I say. "You go. I'll hold them off."

She grabs me by the back of the neck, pulls our heads close together. "We fight together, then."

We stand like that for a moment, as the rain beats against us. "For love," I say.

With that, she turns and charges the men, her spear thrust forward. I follow after her, yelling. My knife finds one man, then another, dropping them both before I am enveloped. I spin and slash a third across the shoulder, then stab a fourth, but they are too many.

I glimpse Aleah amidst their group, running her spear through a man before pivoting to slash another with her knife.

Lightning flashes across the sky. Wind wails. Rain pours. Metal clashes against Aleah's spear, and then something strikes the side of my head.

I fall to my knees, dropping my knife. Aleah cries out and runs toward me, her spear and knife ready. A second blow, harder than the first. Everything goes black.

Thirty-two

When I wake, I feel the hard surface of the deck against my back, the blazing sun blinding my eyes, and the rise and fall of the ocean swells under the boat. Ropes bind my arms, digging into my skin, and straps fastened to pulleys hold me down. A fly buzzes around my face, but I can't move my arms to swat it away. I hear voices from somewhere behind me near the wheel. Water laps against the side of the boat on the swells, and a bottle in a drawer below the deck rolls back and forth with each wave.

"Aleah," I groan.

"He's coming to. Get Syker."

I squint against the sun's glare. A man stands over me, filthy, bearded, teeth rotting, long hair matted. He licks his lips. He says, "You've got meat on your bones."

I'm restrained so well I can only turn my head. The boat is still at anchor dangerously close to the rocky coastline. I see no sign of Aleah.

I hear the footsteps of a man emerge from the darkness below the deck. He steps up into the sunlight and shields his eyes from the glare. "Leave us," he commands.

Bare-chested and broad-shouldered, Syker looks down at me. Despite his age, he's lean with well-defined muscles lining his abdomen and arms. A mane of silver hair sweeps back from a broad forehead, and his face is long, jaw broad, chin like a boot heel. His eyes suggest sadness and loss that, despite myself, I feel in my bones.

"Water?" He kneels over me and holds out a silver flask.

I can't move my hands or arms to take the flask and so study his eyes. They seem to change color from blue to white, but I realize it must be a trick of the glaring sunlight as he shifts his head. Syker holds the flask to my mouth so that I can sip. I refuse.

"What's your name?"

"What did you do with Aleah?"

"What does she matter to you?"

"What did you do to her?" I demand.

"Know something about that one," he says. "She's a deceiver. You can trust nothing she says."

They are dark words that I want to deny because she cared for me. Because she saved my life. Because she gave herself to me. Because I love her.

"You lie," I say.

He gazes out over the ocean beyond the anchored boat. Sighs. "Perhaps," he says.

"What did you do with her?"

"She abandoned you," he says. "Fled. Turned and ran. She leapt into the ocean from up there and is surely dead."

"She did the right thing."

"You deceive yourself now," he says. "How many times have you lied to yourself? If you've spent any time with her at all, then you've felt what I'm telling you is true. In your heart. She doesn't care about others. She only cares about herself."

"Lies."

"It's why she lives like a hermit on the side of a cliff, which no one can reach. Trust your feelings."

"I do trust my feelings."

"Do you?" he says. "What's your name?"

I shake my head. "I don't remember anything from before the island."

He reaches out his hand and places it on my forehead.

"What are you doing?" I wrench my head back and forth trying to move it away from his hand.

"Hold still."

I feel the rough skin of his hand on my forehead, his thumb placed gently over my temple.

"Don't touch me," I say.

After a moment, he removes his hand and looks down at me with newfound appreciation. He says, "You're the reason things are changing. Who are you, that she would take you in? The great deceiver. Why would she? There's something about you that you don't even know about yourself."

"I don't know what you're talking about."

He nods. "I'm sure you don't."

He rises and disappears from my line of sight into the depths below the deck. When he returns a moment later, he holds the silver flask. The sun's rays glint off of it. He kneels beside me and holds the flask to my mouth. I shake it off.

"You should drink," he says, "while there's fresh water to be had."

"You're taking this boat somewhere. Where?"

"You'll see soon enough."

I peer into his eyes. "I know how to sail."

"You?"

"The mast you've built won't last."

He smiles with his sad eyes, a mixture of consideration and condescension that belies the difference in our ages. He is an old man who knows more than I can ever hope to know.

"Tell me, new arrival, how do you know how to sail?"

"You need a lighter wood," I say. "Something that'll bend when the wind roars, or your mast will break and you'll be lost at sea."

Syker glances up at the mast.

I say, "And you need a third more length to move a boat this size at more than a snail's crawl."

His gaze falls on me again. "Clever. Think that'll save you?"

"What if I don't want to be saved?"

He gazes at me with something like pity. He looks up at his followers near the boat's wheel. He motions with his fingers for the men to come, and then he rises.

"Beat him," Syker says, descending below deck. "But don't kill him."

The men take turns kicking, punching, and spitting on me. They laugh and make a competition of it to see if they can knock me unconscious with a kick or punch to my head. The only rules seem to be that they can't use weapons and that I'm not allowed to die.

Otherwise, the beating is without mercy.

Thirty-three

My hands and arms are still bound. My head and ears are covered in buzzing flies. I open my eyes.

They are trying to pull up the anchor.

I wince.

One of the men says, "The one who doesn't bleed awakens."

A wave strikes the vessel broadside, and the men lose their balance. One falls overboard. He cries for help, but no one rescues him. They are all stunned by the force of the ocean, grasping at whatever they can hold onto and staying low for balance on the foredeck. The boat teeters hard on the backside of the swell, and the makeshift mast they've constructed rattles in its boot. The boat comes down and then is hit by another wave. The sail they've raised flaps in the wind, luffing so hard it threatens to tear.

"You fools!" Syker yells from the wheel. "Pull the anchor!"

I watch them. "Won't release. Unless you're on top of it."

One of the men kicks me hard in the side of the ribs.

"Shut your mouth," he says, "or we'll throw you overboard."

"You need to kick a little harder," I say.

Then the man says to the others, "Get over the anchor for it to release."

Syker yells, "Pull!"

Together they haul in the line, pulling the boat inch by inch against the huge swells, until it is almost directly over the anchor.

"It's free!" one of the men shouts. "Turn the boat!"

The wind quickly pushes them toward the rocky coastline, the sail still luffing hard.

"Tighten the boom," I groan, "or we'll all be killed."

"Shut your mouth." The man kicks me again. Then he calls to Syker, "Pull the boom tight! Turn the wheel!"

Syker yells, "Pull the boom tight!"

I watch the flapping sail gradually fill with wind. The sailboat tilts on its keel, gaining momentum, and eases away from the small island and its rocky coastline. The swells coming in from the sea hit the boat's side, sending seaspray up over the deck. The men shout orders at one another. No one knows what they are doing. Bound and strapped to the foredeck, I'm pretty sure I'm going to die.

Syker turns the boat into the wind, and the sail flaps wildly, luffing. The boat stalls out, and the men shout orders at one another.

I feel the vessel turning in the wind, and I sense the boom is about to swing around out of control.

Seaspray and water smash against the side and up over the deck, dousing me, threatening to drown me. I cough and tilt my head up and away from the saltwater rushing over the deck.

The boat turns, the wind behind us, and then the boom swings with tremendous force. It knocks three men overboard, almost certainly killing one who is struck in the head by the sheer weight of the wood. The boom reaches the end of its lines, and the boat starts to tilt more than forty-five degrees. The end of the boom hits the water, and I hear the wood crack. An instant later, the sail rips as a piece of wood pierces through it.

The boat rights itself. Somehow the men manage to haul the lines, bringing the makeshift boom under control. The boat once again takes off at a crawl, but this time the sail is ripped badly and the wind threatens to widen the tear.

The boom has cracked, although it is still in one piece for the moment. Another equally poor turn and the whole thing will come apart, boom, mast, and sail.

"Steady!" Syker yells from the wheel.

The boat glides along past the channel that divides the two islands. Syker holds the wheel. The huge swells beat against the sides.

I wonder if anyone has considered the depth where they're planning to moor the boat and whether the keel will run aground, but I say nothing.

Thirty-four

The boat is still. Dusk settles over the flat water of the natural harbor. Flies buzz around my face, and the chirping of crickets from the woods reaches across the water. I smell smoke, squint, and see a village at the edge of the beach. Still bound to the foredeck, I can barely move.

I close my eyes and concentrate on breathing. My mouth feels like someone has swabbed it with a rotten dish rag.

Footsteps along the gunwale.

"You ready for another beating, freak?"

I squint and see a filthy, emaciated man standing over me. He is shirtless, skin tight over his ribcage, bearded and covered in grime and dirt that lines the creases around his eyes. His shoulder has a nasty cut on it that is not healing well. He grins, and I see his rotten teeth.

The man dunks a bucket over the side of the boat, brings it up, and douses me.

"Drink up, scum."

I hear laughter from men behind me that I can't see. The sun is below the hills to the west of the harbor, and the saltwater on my skin makes me shiver.

"Let me move my arms."

"What's that?"

"My arms," I say. "I need to move them so I can rip you limb from limb."

"Shut your mouth, freak. Killed five of our brothers. Sliced my shoulder. We're going to make you hurt. You can count on that." He spits in my face. "Drink up," he says, and the men laugh again.

Thirty-five

Two nights pass at anchor in the harbor. I drift in and out of consciousness bound to the foredeck. Occasionally one of the men kicks me, stomps me, punches me, or commits acts even more deplorable.

Once or twice a man will lower a bucket over the side of the boat and douse me in saltwater to rinse away the filth. This is not an act of mercy on my behalf, I realize, as much as it is a way of making my smell less intolerable for Syker's men repairing the boat. They continue to haul out water from below deck, which makes clear to me the vessel's leaks are not yet repaired.

On the morning following my second night in the harbor, I wake and see a dozen men emerge from the village on the beach. They carry a new mast on their shoulders. They wade down into the water and then swim with the floating wood.

They bring the new mast parallel to the boat. Men climb aboard and tie ropes along the length of wood. They attach the ropes to pulleys. Then standing to port, they lift the new mast onto the side of the vessel.

I realize they are working better as a team. Syker yells instructions from the helm. His tribe obeys. They are of a single purpose now, and the wind and water are calm in the harbor.

"Lighter wood, freak," one man says to me. "Hope you like it."

Thirty-six

I wake under starlight to the sound of a lone guard on the foredeck whistling to the night. High atop the new mast, the ship's bell clangs as the vessel rotates on its mooring in the gentle breeze. Fires blaze on the beach. The light dances on the calm water.

•••

"Eat this."

Syker kneels over me with a wooden bowl. I open my eyes in the predawn light to see white gruel on the spoon before my lips. He thrusts it into my mouth, and I feel the spoon's wooden texture and taste flavors of animal fat, mint, coconut, fish, and ground meat. I've not eaten in three days.

"Good," he says. "Swallow."

I manage to swallow the mixture without gagging. He holds a flask of water to my mouth. I sip.

We continue this way for several minutes.

"You smell awful," he says.

Of course I smell awful. I've not been allowed to move from my bindings for three days.

"I almost feel sorry for you."

"Want to know what you can do with your 'sorry'?"

"Murderer," he says.

I say nothing.

He nods. My eyes glance at the bowl of food, but he holds it a foot or two away, unreachable by me in my bindings. "To keep a tribe together, we must have laws."

"What are you going to do with me?" I ask.

"I'm grateful for you, actually," he says. "You've confirmed something important."

I stare at him.

He says, "The need for an example of what happens when you break our laws."

He gazes out across the harbor in the early morning light. A thin mist hangs over the calm water. Sounds from the camp come from the beach: roosters crowing, the clang of a metal pot, low and inaudible conversations near one of the fires, water lapping gently on the shoreline.

"Everyone in our village has seen you now," he says. "The embodiment of evil." I say nothing, though the thought crosses my mind that he may be projecting just a bit. He continues, "You're filth, inhuman, and you're bound and under control—as evil should be. Everyone would like to see you die. No one cares for you. No one."

I glare at the man.

"How does that make you feel?" he asks.

"Free me for one minute, and I'll show you how it feels."

"You are the evil one," he says.

I follow his eyes as he looks toward the beach. Children play on the sand with wooden sticks. Two girls and a boy, no more than six years old, turn and see me bound on the foredeck of the boat, Syker kneeling over me with food and water. For an instant, I see myself from their eyes: Syker appearing to give me food and water. The embodiment of evil to these people receiving their leader's kindness. The children, passing no judgment in their gaze from the beach, return to playing with the wooden sticks, chasing one another and laughing.

He says, "We all arrive on this island the same way with good and evil inside of us. We choose. Or fate chooses for us, and we simply act. For our people, you are evil, and this is what happens to evil. This is what happens when you choose the wrong path. You tell me, who's right?"

"There is no right."

"I didn't put myself on this island," he says. "Something else did. Something beyond us. It decides what is right, if only by virtue of what survives."

He breathes deeply, sighs, stirring the remaining gruel in the bowl. He offers the last bit to me. I shake it off. "We'll keep you alive," he says. "You are the way to teach our people what not to do."

A woman approaches, twice as old as me yet not as old as Syker. She holds something in her hands, and he takes it from her.

He turns and holds the life vest before me.

I study it. The vest is faded, dirty, and torn. A shattered emergency locator beacon on the shoulder no longer flashes. One corner has been burned in a fire. A slash across the front has released all of the air long ago. Otherwise it is identical to the one I wore when I first woke at sea.

He unfolds the life vest and points to the markings on the lapel, almost identical to the markings on my life vest.

I study them: JOR. V. 1.04

"What does it mean?"

He shakes his head. "Aleah gave it to me. Said it was the first. Most others have been lost, but they all look the same, except for the last few...symbols. She tell you about this?"

I say nothing.

"Whoever put us here erased everyone's memory, including our ability to read," he says. "Never has the need of knowledge been so important."

I sense something in the old man's speech. It is subtle and maybe means nothing. "I have an idea," I say.

"Yes?"

"The letters say you should let me go."

Syker stares at me. "Do they now?"

"They say if you don't, you are going to be fed to the sharks."

"I could drown you right this moment, and no one would care."

I think about it for a moment. Nod in my restraints.

He hands the life vest back to the woman with a glance that suggests he knows something about the vest that I can't fathom.

Then he gazes calmly at me and says, "We'll show you what evil looks like."

Thirty-seven

That night, something on the water catches my attention. Flotsam gathered in a mass of seaweed floats toward the boat. Against the current. I glance at the lone guard to see if he notices it. But he appears to be dozing. His head bobs an instant and then snaps up. He shudders, trying to keep himself awake. He coughs and clears his throat, and then his head falls slowly forward. His chin rests on his chest.

The seaweed moves closer to the boat.

I hear Syker below deck with a woman: the muffled sound of pleasure. A bottle falls to the floor, laughter, a pause, and then more of the sounds. A breeze picks up and shifts the boat on its mooring. The mass of seaweed moves against the wind as it continues approaching.

Something catches in the guard's throat as he starts to snore. He coughs and sits upright. Spits into the water, complains about his aching back, stands up, feet bare on the deck. He mutters something about the noises coming from below deck.

The guard turns and peers out over the water toward the fire on the beach. He doesn't see the seaweed, and I pretend to sleep. He spits on me. I remain still and pretend to sleep through it all.

Through slitted eyes, I see that the guard notices the seaweed. He grabs a length of wood they use as a boat hook and kneels to try and fish some of it up on the end. Water pours down from the seaweed as he raises it from the surface.

"What is this mess?"

Aleah rises, and her spear impales the guard. He cries out as he falls overboard splashing into the water, sounds loud enough to rouse the attention of Syker and others below deck.

She climbs aboard the boat, draped in a seaweed shawl and carrying a knife and her spear. She approaches me, puts a finger to her lips.

I stare at her in the moonlight. Her face glistening with water. Her hair slicked back. Beautiful.

Syker calls the guard's name from below deck, and when he doesn't reply, Syker curses, shouts at the others, and then emerges from the salon near the wheel half-naked.

"Come on!" Aleah grabs my hand and helps me to my feet. We dive into the water before Syker reaches us. I swim hard.

He shouts, "Get them!" But we are already too far. We swim parallel to the beach and the current works with us, carrying us away. And then, we're back ashore.

"This way." Aleah peels off the seaweed as she runs, leading me up the beach and into the woods.

Thirty-eight

Through the dark woods we run. In the distance, I hear the sound of pursuers, see the glint of torchlight flicker through the trees. She guides me down into a creekbed carved by water coming from the mountain ahead of us.

"If we climb now," she whispers, "we'll be exposed. Come with me." She pulls me under a natural lean-to, a green cave nestled against the creek bank and covered by branches, ferns, and vines.

Water trickles among the rocks at our feet. She touches my face.

"I thought you were dead."

"Quiet," she says. "Their lights."

A group of four men trample into a small clearing not far from the creek. We remain silent.

"Can you see anything?" one of the men asks.

"We'll never find them."

"We should go back to the village."

"Syker will have us whipped if we return with nothing."

"Syker was the one who let them escape."

One of the men holding a torch wanders over to the ditch. He is so close Aleah could spear him, but the man doesn't see her. He scoops water with his free hand, drinks, wipes his mouth, tilts his torch to see better up and down the ditch.

"Tell you what I'd do if I found her," he calls to the others.

"Was she really the first?" another asks.

"I'd teach her what it means to respect a man."

His back is to us. Aleah could lean forward at any moment and drive her spear right through his shoulder blades.

"That's why she left, you know," another says. "She constantly bickered with Syker. She didn't respect him or the moral laws."

That's it. Aleah has had enough. In one smooth movement, she stands and drives her spear through the man's back. He gasps and falls to his knees. His torch hits the ground, and a burst of fire quickly spreads up the bank.

She climbs from the ditch, stepping on the man's writhing body. "You want my respect. Come get it. Then tell me about the moral laws."

The three remaining men all hold torches and weapons. They surround her. I climb from the ditch, taking a knife from the dying man, and sidestep the torch fire that now covers the ground.

I say, "You're all going to die."

One of the men lunges, swinging his torch at Aleah. She ducks. He stumbles forward. Before he can regain his balance, she drives her spear through him, his own momentum killing him. He falls to his knees, clutching at his chest. The other two men look from one to the other, stunned.

Fire now blazes behind us.

She jerks her spear from the man's chest and looks at the other two men. "Tell me again about respect. I've seen your kind come and go and have killed so many of you I've lost count."

First one then the other throws his torch on the ground and runs, fleeing into the wooded darkness.

I watch them retreat.

Once they're out of sight, she turns to me. "Help me put this fire out before it spreads."

Thirty-nine

The waterfall comes from the side of the sandstone cliff through a natural culvert that has opened up from the rain. Aleah leads me by hand to the water, which pours in a clear stream, splashing on the rocks of the tide pool beneath her cave. The sunrise over the ocean paints the clouds red, orange, and gold. The sky is pale with just a few stars still visible in the west, and the sea is a deep shade of blue.

Barefoot and covered in mud and plant debris, she steps under the waterfall.

I watch as the mud and dirt wash from her hair and face, racing down over her clothes. She leans her head back and lets the water rinse her completely.

"You saved my life. Again." I step toward her. "I thought you were dead, Aleah."

She looks at me, touches my face, fingertips caressing my cheek, the line of my brows. I return the favor, unable to not touch her, running my thumbs over her skin.

"Kiss me," she says.

I pull her to me, press my lips to hers. Water races down her shoulders and back, and I feel her breasts through the wet fabric of her shirt. Her hands slide down my body, grab my hips, pull me into her, grinding her body against mine. Her lips move to my jaw, my neck, my shoulder, as my hands drift over the curve at the small of her back.

She tugs at the waistband of my pants. "I can't believe we made it out of there." She slowly slides them down past my thighs until they hit the ground. "Alive."

"Do you have any idea what you do to me?" My voice is low, thick with desire.

"I have an idea," she whispers in my ear, sending a surge of heat straight to my groin, "of what I'd like to do to you."

She strips off her soaked shirt and throws it on the rocks away from the waterfall. Finally, her skin is flush against mine, and I ease my fingertips into the waistband of her shorts.

"Do you trust me now?" she asks.

"How could I have ever doubted?" I kiss her neck, trace my tongue over her collarbone, down to her chest.

"Because I'm becoming convinced you were right." She gasps.

My lips move to the soft skin of her breasts, pulling one tip into my mouth, as my fingers move up from her navel and cup the other in my hand, kneading firmly.

"And that we need to leave the island."

"Together," I say and move to the other breast.

She sucks in a breath. "Together." Strokes me up and down. "We will. Find a way."

Forty

That evening at sunset, three drones approach the mouth of the cave. I rise slowly. Aleah grabs her spear.

One of the drones separates from the others and comes to rest on the ground at the cave entrance. Red, yellow, and green lights flash along its sides. Legs extend from its body. Metal feet click and slip on the damp, rocky cave floor. At first, it moves cautiously, slipping and righting itself as it approaches. Lenses on its body scan the walls, the ceiling, Aleah, me. As it moves toward us, I run forward and kick it, knocking it on its back. The legs flail about in the air like tentacles. Then, they swing down, and the machine flips itself over.

A second drone lands at the entrance, and it too extends metal legs from its body. It scurries to the side of the first, as another limb emerges from the back of the drone's body. Only, this one curls up and over like a scorpion's tail, a long needle affixed to its tip.

"Careful," I say just as a needled tail extends from the first machine. It moves toward me. "Look out!"

The second drone scuttles toward her, the tail extending. She swings her spear at the tail. Sparks flash. The entire unit is knocked to its side, but it quickly rights itself. I back away from the first drone, my eyes scanning the floor for something to throw at it. I grab a rock from the floor by the cave wall and slam it down on the body just as the needle sweeps toward me, barely missing my leg.

The blow stuns the machine. It shakes and beeps as if resetting its circuitry. Then it turns and rushes at Aleah, joining the second drone as they try to block her against the wall.

She swings her spear back and forth, growling at them. "Stay away from me! Get back!"

They're moving slowly now, methodically, trying to cage her in. I've got to distract them, so I scoop up pebbles and dirt from the floor and rush toward them. "Come get me!"

The drones pivot and turn their attention to me, moving faster now, forcing me back against the wall. "Aleah, go!" I throw the dirt and rocks at their lenses.

"Go now," I shout, "I've got them!"

Aleah watches the third drone come to rest on the floor near the cave entrance, and it too extends legs and a scorpion-like tail. All three spread out and come toward us.

I bend to drag one hand along the floor beside me, gathering as many rocks from the cave floor as I can. I strike the closest drone, cracking a lens, but the other two continue to advance.

I sense they're improving their coordination. They seem to be learning at lightning speed, processing our counterattacks and responding better with each move.

I've got one last large rock in my hand, and I throw with all my strength, striking the damaged drone so hard I smash its top. The other two hesitate this time, and Aleah and I dash by them toward the entrance to the cave.

The damaged drone sputters and sparks, but one of the others trips Aleah. She stumbles at the cave entrance and almost goes over the edge. Her spear clatters to the ground. Her head hits the rocky floor.

I kneel and try to help her stand. "Come on!" I look back into the cave. I grab her spear and swing it at the advancing machines.

I hear behind me the roar of the ocean beating against the rocks. With the spear in hand, I approach one of the drones.

"Back off!" I thrust the spear. The tip dents its metal body, but that only seems to anger it. The scorpion tail lashes at me, sending me backward, as the second drone sweeps its tail, striking me broadside, knocking me to my knees. The needle tip doesn't puncture my skin, but the spear clatters once more to the ground.

Aleah grabs it, rolls over, and thrusts it up, deep into the body of the drone. Her body convulses, and I crawl toward her as the impaled drone writhes in spasms of mechanical sparks and smoke. The third drone freezes, its camera lenses assessing the casualties.

I kneel by Aleah. "You alright?"

She moans, and her eyes squint at me. "What happened?"

"Electrical shock, I think. Can you move? Can you get up?"

"Jordan!" she cries.

Rotors spinning, the third drone pushes off the ground and flies at my head. I leap to my feet, reach out, and grab it, but the momentum knocks me backward.

Over the edge.

Clutching the drone, I tumble through the air. Above me, Aleah cries out, "No! Jordan, no!"

The drone's tail flails wildly, still trying to sting me, and I slam its body into the cliff face as I plummet. The machine screams, sparks, then bursts into flames.

Aleah yells my name from above.

That's the last thing I hear before the rocky shoreline rushes toward me.

Forty-one

"You can't be human." The voice comes to me in the darkness.

Flashing light. Whirring, buzzing. Pain. The roar of surf crashing on the rocks. The spray of saltwater on my face. The warmth of a hand on my cheek, caressing me. Cool water washing up over the rocks, soaking my skin. The water recedes, and I open my eyes to see her hover over me with the dusky sky as her backdrop. A few stars have emerged in the heavens.

"Everything hurts."

She blinks. "How are you alive?"

"My neck—" I sit up, and she takes my hands in hers. She is on her knees beside me. The water comes up over the rocks once more and touches our skin. "Stiff."

"You have a cut here, at your hairline." Her fingers inspect my scalp. "But it's barely bleeding."

I hold out my arms and study my hands. Not even a scratch. Her brow furrows with concern. "Help me stand."

"What are you?"

I glance at the remains of the last drone, scorched and scattered in pieces among the rocks. "'Lucky' comes to mind."

"That's not what I mean." She just stares at me as I walk around getting my bearings. "Jordan?"

"Yeah."

"How in the world?"

"There will be more drones coming for us in the night."

Forty-two

"That fall is not the first thing." I look around the night-darkened cave at the two destroyed drones, one with the spear still impaled in it.

Aleah retrieves her bota and fills it with water from the cask. She cuts a piece of meat, eats, and scans her surroundings. She won't look at me.

"On the raft," I say, "when I first woke, the kid tried to kill me. He cut my arm." She glances at me. "First, the blade barely broke my skin," I say. "Then, the cut he made... It healed in hours."

She says nothing.

"How do you explain that?"

She shakes her head. "I can't."

"On the boat," I say, "Syker's men beat me over and over. I didn't bleed. I didn't even bruise." I stare at her in the darkness of the cave, colorless in the dim light of night. "How could I survive that fall?" I watch her and think I see something flicker in her eyes.

"They must've done something to you. I don't know. Reinforced you. Skin and bones." I let that sink in a moment. "But you're right about one thing," she continues. "We can't stay here tonight. There will definitely be more drones."

She reaches forward and takes the spear in her hands, then wrenches it from the dead drone. It makes a scraping sound as it emerges from the metal body, but it doesn't shock her. It's truly dead.

She holds the spear in her hand. She appraises it a moment, running her fingers along its shaft.

"Why am I here, Aleah?"

She looks into my eyes, studies my face. "I wish I could tell you."

"What am I?"

She looks away.

Forty-three

I don't sleep well. Even after the walk across the island at night. We settle in some brush along the creek. Aleah falls asleep fast. I wake in fits and starts, alert to any sound. I rise a few hours before sunrise and walk down to the water, listening to the gentle rush of the creek flowing over rocks.

Scanning the forest in the moonlight, I lift my face to the breeze rustling through the trees. I feel despair come over me, my mind swamped, tortured by all that I've seen, all that I've experienced. Tortured by my own uncertainty of who I am, what I am, whether there is any meaning for my existence. I close my eyes. *Why am I here? Why are any of us here? Who is doing this to us?*

I kneel, reach my hands into the cool water, think of the fall, and touch my head where the cut has healed. My entire body should be shattered, broken. And yet... I can't be human. Yet what I feel inside is an emotional hell that seems all too human.

I splash water on my face and run my hands through my hair. Except for the distant sound of the surf and the rush of water in the creek, everything is quiet. Peaceful. It's all a lie. I tell myself. Everything. I turn and see Aleah sleeping in the camouflage of foliage not far away.

"Just focus on her," I whisper. "Channel your anxiety into love for her. It's the only thing that's real."

I go to her, kneel at her feet, and watch her sleep. Her eyes move back and forth under her lids, and her fingers are curled up together like the petals of a flower. An owl hoots, breaking the silence. I turn to see if I can locate it. It hoots again, and I follow the sound. I find it soothing, if haunting.

Finally, I stop in a clearing near the creek. I spot the owl on a branch. The great bird is motionless in my presence, and I can only see its contours in the night against the backdrop leaves, branches, and distant stars. Somehow it calms me. I breathe deeply, the cool night air soothing in my lungs. The owl is real, I tell myself. The owl is real. The trees are real. The water is real. Not everything is a lie.

After a few moments, the bird pivots its head, ducks, and then leaps off the branch. Its wings spread and flap and sweep through the air, and I watch it vanish into the darkness of the forest upstream.

I wait a moment more and then return to Aleah and lie beside her on the ground. I reach my hand to touch her hip.

She startles awake. "What?"

I whisper, "Everything's okay."

She curls into me, murmurs, "I love you, Jordan."

I don't respond, and soon she snores lightly. I know she won't recall this exchange in the morning.

Forty-four

At daybreak, I wake to the sound of running footsteps and huffing breath coming from upstream. Aleah grabs her spear and motions for me to join her in the thick foliage beyond our site.

"The fire," I whisper.

"No time."

We hide in the shrubs and grasses at the edge of the clearing, burying ourselves amidst the weeds.

Two figures emerge from upstream. They run through the water and spot smoke from the fire. They come up the bank.

I recognize the man and woman I saved.

"Fire." The guy points.

The young woman sees it and quickly scans the clearing. "Look alive. Someone's here. I can feel it."

My heart hammers in my chest as I study them from the tall grass. The guy's skin is the color of walnut. His thick hair has grown longer since I last saw him. It is uneven, as though he's trimmed it with a knife. His eyes are quick, intelligent, and the color of sand. He is lean and muscular, and I see that his scar tissue has healed into welts over his dark skin.

He carries a mace the length of his arm. He notices something on the ground, kneels, and calls for the young woman.

"What is it?"

"Tracks." He touches the earth with his finger and then looks up in our direction.

I realize they can't see me and Aleah but that they sense our presence in the grass.

"Who's there?" he shouts, rising to his full posture.

I find a throwing rock. Aleah nods, and we rise together.

"What is your name?" I clutch the rock in my hand.

The guy glares at me. "You."

"Are you alone?" the young woman asks.

"What is your name?" I ask.

"My name is Wren," she says. "This is Marcus."

Silence follows as Aleah shifts the spear in her throwing hand. "Put your weapon down."

"You first," Marcus says.

"I can hit a bird at forty paces with this spear."

"You threatening us?" Marcus stands tall.

"Take it easy, both of you," I say. "There's plenty of people on this island who want to kill us. We don't need to kill ourselves."

Marcus glares at me. "Tell her to back off."

"She doesn't listen to me," I say.

Wren looks from Aleah to me and then nods at Marcus. "We've just seen an entire tribe wiped out over the past two days."

Aleah's eyes go wide. "No. Where? Who?"

"The village is still burning," Wren says. "We're the only two to make it out alive."

No one says anything for a moment. I watch as Aleah processes what Wren has said. A bird chirps on a branch over the creek. The stream babbles over the rocks.

Suddenly, Aleah throws her spear faster than any of us can react. The steel whistles through the air, strikes a metal loop in the chain of Marcus's mace, and then drives the mace from his hand and into a tree behind him.

He looks down at his empty hand, at the mace pinned to the wood, and then back at Aleah.

"You're going to need to learn to listen," she says.

Forty-five

We make camp that night on a hillside amidst a stand of boulders not far from the creek. Marcus scowls at Aleah who offers food to Wren.

"How'd you come to be in the clearing that day?" I ask. "With Syker's men."

Wren and Marcus exchange a look. She hands him some of the food that Aleah has given her. Marcus sniffs the dried meat.

"Why don't you tell me about yourself first?" He takes a bite.

"Wish I knew," I say. "I have no memory from before this island."

"Join the club." Marcus chews. "I don't remember anything either."

I peer at Aleah who sits with her arms draped over her knees, her spear on the ground at her side. She sips water from her bota, watches us.

"I woke at sea in a life vest," I say. "No memory of who I am or how I came to be here."

Marcus listens, watches. Alert.

"There was a kid with me at first. Younger than you. Shark took him. He had something wrong with his head."

"What do you mean?"

"Some kind of neurological disorder," I say. "I tried to save him. He died in my arms."

He swears. "I'm sorry, man."

"She found me by the creek." I nod toward Aleah. "Not long after that. After I made it to the island."

Wren asks, "So you two didn't arrive together?"

I shake my head. "No."

"You've seen him then?" Marcus asks.

"Syker?"

"I'm going to kill him if it's the last thing I do," he says.

"What did he do to you?"

Marcus leans back, resting on his outstretched arms. He glances at Wren, then up, gazing into the distance.

"Us," he says. "What he did to us."

"Water?" Aleah offers.

Marcus waves it off. "Dude is evil. He needs to die."

Wren takes the water from Aleah and sips. "Thank you."

"I'll do whatever it takes to kill him," Marcus says.

I look hard into his eyes. He spits to his side, glances at Aleah who has started to sharpen her knife with a smooth stone from the creek.

"Well," I say, "that's something we have in common."

Forty-six

In the morning, Aleah and I follow Marcus and Wren through the forest to the ruins of the fishing village. Thick smoke clings to the shoreline, where huts lie in ruin, bodies strewn across the sand. We scan the area from the woods.

"The drones hit us two nights in a row." Marcus studies the remains. I count twenty-three dead. He continues, "The first night caught us completely by surprise."

"You came here after Syker's men tried to kill you?"

"This tribe was peaceful," Wren says. "Fishermen mostly, they took us in. Accepted us."

I hear something from one of the charred huts.

We're silent. I listen carefully to the gentle lapping of water along the shoreline, the crackle of embers from the village. Smell the scent of smoke. Then, I hear it again.

"Someone's still alive," I whisper.

"That's Grady's hut," Marcus says. "The blind man."

I leave the forest and walk out onto the beach.

"He doesn't listen to me," Aleah says.

I step past bodies covered in flies. Flick open my knife. Approach the blackened hut from which I heard the sound. The village is so thick with smoke, it makes my eyes water and I cough. The smell of death fills my nostrils, putrid, rotting meat.

The door frame has collapsed in on itself. Smoke drifts from the wood. I fight off a feeling of nausea at the odor and peer inside.

A man lies face down, his head turned to one side as though looking at something small on the floor. The man's hair and clothes are singed, and his feet are bare and bloody.

"Brother," I say. "You alive?"

The man's fingers wriggle.

"Water," he groans.

I glance back across the village to the forest beyond the beach, where Aleah, Wren, and Marcus stay hidden.

I enter the hut and kneel beside the man. "Can you roll over?"

"My. Legs."

I help him to roll over and prop a rag under his head. His clothes are crisp with dried blood. Parts still damp. He is nearly bled out. Skin pale, cool to the touch. I fan flies away from his face and see the glassy eyes of a blind man.

"Here." I unscrew the cap of my canteen and put it to the man's mouth. He sips, coughs.

"Can't move," he groans. "My legs."

"Just take it easy."

"More."

I tilt the canteen to his mouth. I reckon that he will surely die here in this remote hut on an island of which none of us understand the purpose, with identities none of us know. That his life amounts to only the haziest speculation as to why he exists at all.

"How can I help you?" I ask. "How can I ease your suffering?"

He groans something I can't discern. I lean closer. He wheezes, his breath raspy and labored. He reaches up and touches my face.

"Take it easy," I say again. "Hang in there."

"You are," the blind man says.

I shake my head, not understanding.

"You are—" He coughs. Clears his throat. Calms. Goes silent.

"I am?" I say.

He reaches a frail hand out and touches my nose, my forehead, my chin.

"—*the* Jordan."

His hand slides down my face, falls to the ground. He exhales. It's nothing more than a whisper. I press my fingers on his bony wrist. No pulse.

Footsteps approach the hut. "Is he?" Aleah asks from the doorway.

I stare at him and shake my head. "Dead."

"Did he say anything?"

I'm holding the man's hand, turning it over in my own, studying it as if it held the answers. "What he said makes no sense."

Marcus and Wren join her in the doorway. "What happened?"

Aleah looks at them. "You know him?"

"Grady," Wren says. "He was kind to us."

"What did he say?" Marcus asks.

I fold Grady's hand over his chest and slowly rise. I look from Marcus to Wren to Aleah. "He wanted water."

"Water." Aleah studies me.

"I gave him a sip of my water."

Forty-seven

The stone structure is situated on a hillside. We discover it at nightfall. For a long while, we've moved through the forest that borders the harbor. No one says a word, and only the occasional sound of an owl breaks the silence. Sweat beads on my face, and I wipe the back of my hand across my brow.

Under the moonlight, we circle the thing, a stone tower covered in moss and vines, rising into the forest canopy.

"What is this?" I ask.

Aleah shakes her head. "I've never been here. Look, there's a door."

"Careful." Marcus uses a stick to clear spiderwebs from the doorway.

"You're not going in there," Wren says.

"I'll go first." I enter and find the ground inside covered in debris, vines, logs, leaves, and husks of dead insects. A spiral stairwell across the room climbs up and around the inside wall.

"How old do you figure this is?" I ask.

Aleah steps inside and goes to a rotted chair and broken table. "Careful," she says. "Might be snakes."

"Can you stay where I can see you?" Wren asks from the doorway.

Aleah grabs the chairback, and something slithers from under the table into a hole in the wall.

Marcus approaches the stairwell. "Steel."

He tests the first step. It holds his weight.

"You going up that?" Aleah asks.

"Marcus, don't," Wren says. "Please."

I peer up the stairwell and see that the stairs lead to a room at the top of the tower. Even by moonlight, the windows in the room provide ample illumination.

"Seems stable enough." Marcus tentatively climbs a few more steps, winding his way up higher along the wall.

"I can't see you!" Wren says, her voice laced with panic.

I look at Aleah as if to ask, *You coming?*

"You two go ahead," she whispers. "I'll stay with her."

The stairwell is sturdily built, the steel fashioned into the stone wall. It holds my weight, and a few moments later, Marcus and I reach the top. Four windows are evenly spaced around the room. Wooden beams hold the ceiling in place.

"Look." He points out one of the windows.

The trees block most of the view, but the boat floats in the moonlight on the tranquil water near Syker's village.

"It's still there," I say.

"Is that a campfire? On the beach?"

"Looks like it."

"Why would the drones attack the fishing village," he asks, "but not Syker's?"

Aleah calls from downstairs. "Guys, I might've found something. Come help."

We descend the stairs to the ground floor.

"What is it?" I ask.

Aleah taps the floor with her spear. "Listen."

She walks around the room, poking at the ground.

"The boat's still on the water. We could see it from up there."

"You hear that?"

I shake my head. "Did you hear what I said? Syker's village is undamaged. They haven't been attacked."

"Over here," she says. "Help me clear this away."

Wren joins her now. Together we clear the dirt and debris from the spot she's found. The floor is made of wood. Rotted with age and exposure to the forest. She drives her spear into it, and to my surprise, the clang of metal-on-metal rings out.

"Help me." She points. "See the seams? It's a trap door."

She uses her spear to pry it open. The hinges come away from the wood like rotten teeth, and we all stare at a double-sided cellar door made of reinforced steel. It has been hidden under the floorboards.

The door is held together by a sliding rectangular vault handle secured with a padlock, which itself is wrapped and sealed in a plastic bag.

"What is that?" Wren points to two symbols painted on either door. The perimeter of the circles are painted black. Inside each, three yellow and three black triangles meet at a small black dot in the center.

I ask Aleah, "You've never seen this?"

"What do you think?"

Marcus tears away the plastic bag that has kept the padlock dry. "Stand back." He motions for space, then strikes the padlock with his mace. The sound is loud. He kneels and inspects the lock. Stands. Swings once more.

"Too loud," I say.

He kneels again. "Let me see the spear."

Aleah does not give it to him.

Hand out, he says, "C'mon. Let me see it."

Her mouth tightens in a straight line, but she hands it to him. He inserts the tip into the loop of the shackle. It fits snugly, and he slides the spear further into the loop, then stands, using it like a lever.

"Stand back." He wrenches the spear upward and the padlock cracks. He kneels, clears the lock away completely, and then hands the spear back to Aleah. "Help me lift these."

An iron handle is welded to both cellar doors. The metal hinges on one side squeal with age, but together we lift the first one, then the second. The doors are thick and heavy.

I stare into the darkness below.

"You know what this is?" Marcus says. "Reinforced steel. Bag over the lock."

I say, "Doesn't look that old."

"Before any of us were here," Aleah says.

We stand over the hole in the floor and look at one another. A metal access ladder is attached to the wall and descends about four body lengths to a floor. Marcus is the first down. When he reaches the bottom, he looks up. "It's dry. Cool and dry down here."

"Can you see anything?" I ask.

"Too dark."

He steps away from the ladder, out of sight. Wren says, "Marcus?"

"Wait a minute," he calls out.

"What is it?" I ask.

He returns to the access ladder, takes a few steps up, and hands something to us. A thick, white wax candle. Never before used. I look at Aleah in the moonlight coming from the windows. "Can you light it?"

Aleah glances around. "Wren, help me gather some kindling."

She uses her knife to cut wicker from the old chair's back and seat, while we gather twigs, leaves, and branches.

"Thanks." She shreds the wicker using her fingernails and knife until she's built a dry nest. She carries it outside and fashions stones into a small fire pit against the tower wall. She uses her flint to strike the back of her blade.

The nest of dry wicker catches a spark. She breathes on it gently until a flame emerges.

"Here." Wren gives her the candle, and Aleah lights the wick. She looks up at me.

"Let's see what else is down there."

Forty-eight

Marcus waits for us at the bottom of the ladder. I go down, then Aleah. Wren stays in the tower at ground level. I notice how cool the cellar is. The floors are made of smooth concrete, fine enough that a marble could roll from one end to the next. The walls are rough to the touch, and the acoustics suggest they are dense and thick.

"Bomb shelter," Aleah whispers.

"What do you mean?" I spy a doorway to a second room. The air is dry and redolent of flour and gasoline. Chrome metal storage cabinets run the length of the room, and in the back corner stands a small canvas cot large enough for one person. Packages of stored food lie inside the first cabinet. Canned beans, pork, and beef stew. Powdered milk. We find large sacks of flour in another. Eight total.

"I mean someone could stay down here for a long time." She discovers metal cookware, plates, forks, knives, and spoons. Dishrags and soap.

Marcus takes the candle toward the door. Opens it. Steps inside to find two large containers that stand shoulder height. Simple hand-turned valves at the bottom of the tanks near the floor function as spigots. I turn one, scoop a handful, smell and then taste it.

I look up at them. "Water."

Aleah swears.

"Tastes good. Clean."

"Clean water?" Marcus kneels and drinks some.

"I can't see you!" Wren calls from the opening in the ceiling in the other room.

"Everything's cool," Marcus calls out. "We're right here. We found water."

Two additional sleeping cots lie in the second room and an oval-shaped woven rug covers the center of the floor. I lift it. Nothing underneath.

"What do you make of this?" I point at a machine in the corner with a black flex pipe that connects to a vent in the ceiling.

"Ventilation." Marcus flips a switch on the front. A soft whirring sound begins, and lights, running around the edges of the ceiling, flicker on.

We all look up, transfixed. "What's powering it?" I ask.

An instant later, we hear a motor come on inside a cabinet beside the machine. I open it and find a generator encased in a chrome housing not unlike the metal suitcase I'd found when I first woke at sea.

Stenciled on the exterior are words from which I can derive no meaning: NORAD SHIELDED MIL-188-885.

Exhaust pipes rise from the chrome housing into the ceiling inside the cabinet. Stacked on shelves are portable fuel tanks made of similar chrome metallic material.

I lift one and place it on the floor in the middle of the room on the oval rug. I remove the cap, and the sweet dizzying smell of gasoline wafts out of the container with an audible release that suggests pressurization. "They've stored this in such a way as to preserve it. This fuel is still good."

Aleah thumps several of the containers on the shelves inside the cabinet. "They're full."

I glance from the containers to her.

"Careful," she says to Marcus. "That's enough gasoline to blow us all up."

135

Marcus steps back from the container. "Good point."

Wren calls, "Everything alright down there? I'm getting kind of nervous."

Marcus turns to me and Aleah. "Wait here. I'm going to help her down."

Forty-nine

"Why would we ever leave here?" Wren asks.

I watch as she opens cabinet after cabinet inside the cellar. Together we find a small propane stove near the ventilation system with two burners. We find clothes and flashlights and batteries. We find enough food to last the four of us months.

"Clean water," Wren says. She begins washing her face and hands with a rag, soap, and a large bowl. She scrubs intensely. I glance at Aleah and nod without saying a word.

She says to her, "Tell me what you're thinking, Wren."

"There's dirt in my skin."

Aleah watches her for another minute. I look at Marcus. He stares at Aleah and Wren. "Wren." Aleah places her hand on Wren's to soothe her.

"Don't touch me."

"Look at me," she says.

"There's dirt," Wren says. "Can't you see it? I'm just trying to get clean so I can cook."

Aleah removes her hand, and Wren continues to scrub herself fiercely with the rag. Marcus steps toward her. "Wren, you're going to hurt yourself."

"What difference does it make?" Wren says. "Why don't you tell me why it matters if I hurt myself? I'm filthy. I've never been so filthy!"

I let Marcus deal with Wren and decide to set up a propane stove. I light it, realizing I know how to do this. I find a pot and can opener. I open a can of beef stew, then warm it in the pot over the small flame. The ventilation system pulls away exhaust from the burner.

A few minutes later, I ladle the stew into bowls and hand them to Wren, Aleah, and Marcus. The four of us look at one another, none of us knows what to say.

"Thank you." Wren wipes away tears from her eyes, looks at me, then Marcus. "I'm just very scared."

"You're not the only one," Marcus says, reaching out to run a knuckle across her cheek.

Wren lifts a spoon to her mouth. She chews. Swallows. Looks at us. "The things he did to me," she says.

"Syker?" Aleah asks.

"I feel broken. I want *those* memories erased. What he did to me...and to Marcus."

"I don't know if it helps to hear this," Aleah says, "but I know what he does. I know what he tried to do to me."

"Yeah?"

"Yeah."

"I'm sorry," I say, "both of you. I wish I knew a way to make it right."

Marcus looks at me, holds my gaze, his expression hard, determined. "We *will* find a way to make this right. We have to."

•••

I walk around the cellar looking through the cabinets. I find a crate of clear glass bottles. I finish the stew and then pull the crate down onto the floor. I open a cabinet that contains rags.

I look from the rags to the crate of empty bottles.

Marcus stands in the doorway. "What're you doing?"

I take one of the rags and one of the clear glass bottles, and I wind the rag tight and stuff it into the hole at the top of the bottle.

I hold it up. Marcus watches my movement. "Help me see if there are others," I say, pulling the rag from the bottle and then stuffing it into another.

Marcus finds another crate in the cabinet beside the first one. I pick it up and look into his eyes.

"This changes things."

"All of Syker's huts are made of wood."

"They'll burn."

"Exactly."

Marcus follows as I carry the crate to the second room with the ventilation system and the fuel containers. Marcus follows me. Wren and Aleah look at the crate and the bottles, which rattle as I set them on the floor. From the cabinet with the cookware, I find a plastic funnel. I sit on the floor between the crate of glass bottles and the gasoline. I remove one of the rags from atop the crate with the bottles. I open the fuel container. The other three watch me, spellbound.

"Need a bowl," I say.

Wren hands me one.

"Perfect," I say.

I take one glass bottle and set it in the middle of the steel serving bowl.

"Can you help me pour this?" I ask Aleah.

She studies me and seems to realize what I'm up to. I straddle the large canister, tilting it toward the serving bowl and the clear glass bottle. A bit spills. I clean the exterior of the glass bottle with the rag and then sop up the excess.

I hold it up in the light. The liquid swishes around inside, but the rag effectively plugs the hole on top. The smell of gasoline is intense, even with the ventilation system.

"We should do the rest outside," I say.

Aleah looks from the bottle of gasoline into my eyes.

She says, "Brilliant."

STACEY COCHRAN

In the end, I construct fourteen gasoline bottle bombs. I fill and plug them outside the tower while the others eat and drink and clean up as they never have before on the island.

Wren, Marcus, and Aleah sleep on the cots, which they bring up from the cellar and place on the ground floor inside the tower. I rest on the ground in a hidden spot in the forest surrounding the tower. Someone needs to be outside, guarding the others. I try to doze, but every sound, every twitch and turn of a tree branch, every forest animal chirping or rustling in the night disturbs me. Finally, I abandon hope that I will sleep at all.

Fifty

We walk single file and silent through the woods. I'm in front, followed by Wren, Marcus, and Aleah bringing up the rear, spear in hand. We maintain three body lengths between us. Roosters crow from Syker's village. We are close enough that I can smell the smoke from cooking fires.

Sweat trickles down my back and beads on my forehead. I wipe my brow with the back of my hand. My nerves feel like cactus needles pressed along my spine. I raise my fist, bringing the group to a halt.

I pivot, look at the others, and point through the trees.

The village lies below us, and the forest descends the hillside affording just enough clearance to see the huts on the sand.

"They're completely undamaged," I whisper.

Marcus's face takes on a hard look. "That's going to change."

"The boat." Wren points. "One person above deck."

"There are more people below," I say. "Four cabins total."

"Think it's ready to sail?" Aleah asks.

"Sitting high on the water like that. Mast in place. Yeah."

"When then?" Wren looks up at me.

"Middle of the night," I say. "When most of them are sleeping."

Fifty-one

Clouds drift above, shadowing the new moon. The water in the harbor is warm. A light breeze ripples the surface. I swim silently.

Now that we're on the verge of the attack, I doubt myself. I worry about the safety of my friends. I turn to check on them and see Aleah's hand rise in response. I glance up. The cloud cover is a stroke of good luck. The surface of the harbor is black as pitch.

Wren is behind Aleah, swimming silently as well. I'll be the first to reach the boat, which I can see is guarded on deck by one man.

It makes me nervous. Queasy.

When the first bottle bomb goes off onshore, the man on the boat stares for a few seconds as if trying to process what could've caused the fire. He doesn't start yelling until the second one explodes next to a hut a little further down the beach.

"Fire!" he yells. "Fire!"

A third bomb goes off as we near the vessel. I climb aboard from the stern as a fourth explosion lights up the treeline near the huts.

People are rushing out into the darkness, trying to make sense of the explosions.

Someone shouts from the beach, "Ambush!"

I help Aleah and then Wren onboard. Water pours off me onto the fiberglass floor. We've been spotted. The guard comes toward us, spear held high. Aleah clashes with him, metal on metal. I take the man's knees out with a kick. He screams in pain and falls awkwardly forward and then tumbles overboard with a splash.

Another of Syker's men emerges from below deck, his head an easy target. Aleah swings her spear like a bat. It makes a whooshing sound, slicing through the air before it strikes the side of his head with a dull thud. The man grunts and collapses forward. I grab him by the arm, drag him up the steps, and dump him overboard.

I look at Wren and point to the anchor. She nods and moves forward to begin pulling it. Another bottle bomb explodes on the beach, igniting another hut. I focus on the men below deck. Because of the darkness in the salon and cabin, I can see nothing from above the companionway.

From the front of the boat, I can tell Wren's done her job as I hear the metal clatter on the forward deck, the anchor's chain and rope piling on the floor. I hear her padding to the mainsail and turn to see Aleah in position at the wheel.

As the canvas rises up the mast, the boom swings slowly to starboard with the faint breeze on the harbor. I stand over the opening to the hatch waiting for Syker and his men. The boat circles the harbor and starts toward the opening out toward the ocean.

On the beach, Syker's village is ablaze. The fire has spread among the trees at the edge of the sand and multiple huts have turned into infernos. I'm done waiting. "Come on!" I roar at the men hiding below deck. "The village is on fire!"

Suddenly three men emerge from the dark like roaches and rush up the steps toward me. I use the spear I've taken from the guard and swing down hard on the first one. I strike the man across the shoulder, but behind him, the second grabs the spear. I yank it back, and the two men come up into the cockpit. The third stands on the steps.

"Wren!" Aleah shouts.

I swing the spear again, but the man I struck on the shoulder ducks. His partner grabs the metal and pulls me toward him, but I wrench the spear back as hard as I can, and the man falls forward, bracing himself on one knee. Wren kicks him hard in the back, and he falls flat, rolling toward the side of the boat.

Aleah leaves the wheel and pushes the man overboard. He lands with a splash but manages to hold onto the side. With a grunt, she stomps on his grasping fingers. The other man reaches the steering wheel and spins it hard. The boat swings to port, and the man clinging to the side falls away. I catch a brief flash of him treading water as the boat races onward.

Aleah rushes back to the wheel, as the boat veers toward land. He's gripping the wheel with both hands, and she launches herself at him, punching his nose with all her strength. Blood sprays everywhere, and he loses his grip on the wheel and staggers back. She's on him again, pushing and punching until he topples overboard.

The one man left rushes forward, nearly tripping on the mainsheet ropes. He grabs Aleah from behind. She cries out, and at the same time bends forward and flips the man over her shoulder. Somehow, he manages to stay on his feet. He grabs her arm and flings her hard. She hits the steering wheel. The boom swings and strikes her across the back of her shoulders, sending her over the edge and into the water, but not before Wren dives across the deck and grabs Aleah's leg.

The man barks out a laugh. "Two for one! Got you both now."

"Hey!" I shout.

The man turns, and I thrust the spear at him but he spins sideways so it misses. But his footing is unstable, and I rush him, pushing him backward and overboard. I hit the deck hard.

"Help!" Wren cries. I crawl over to her side, grab Aleah's leg, and together, Wren and I pull her onto the boat.

Aleah rolls to her stomach and coughs up water. I run to the wheel and turn the ship back toward the open ocean.

Wren points. "There he is!"

144

I can see a figure heading toward us, powerful arms cutting through the water on a course to intersect with the boat.

She waves her arms and jumps up and down. "Marcus! Marcus!"

Behind Marcus, on the shore, Syker's village is ablaze. I see people escaping up the beach toward the island's interior. Others douse buckets of water on the inferno that has overtaken their grass and wooden huts.

"Watch the hatch," I say. "Syker may still be down there!"

I let the sails luff by steering toward Marcus and into the wind. The boat slows.

"I've got him," Wren says.

She and Aleah, now recovered enough to help, reach over the side and grab Marcus's arm. They pull him out of the water and onto the deck, where he lies on his back, chest heaving.

"We need to check the cabins," I say. "Syker hasn't appeared yet."

Marcus pulls himself up to sit against the side of the boat. Wren drops to her knees and pulls him into her arms. He wraps his arms around her, strokes her hair, whispers in her ear. I turn away to steer the boat out of the harbor toward the open sea beyond the island.

"I'll do it," Marcus says, finally, starting to stand.

"Aleah, can you take the wheel? We'll go below to clear the cabins."

Aleah takes my place at the wheel, and Marcus and I head below.

"Watch my back," I tell him. He nods and follows me without another word.

The boat moves around quite a bit on the larger swells as we put distance between us and the island. Before we go below, I fasten the lines. The vessel angles slightly, heading off the wind. Seaspray splashes along the side.

I step toward the companionway, swaying a bit. I ready my knife and then step below deck. In the darkness, I breathe the stale, humid air of the enclosed space. I steady myself, my feet shoulder-width apart, and I let my eyes adjust.

No one in my immediate vicinity.

I hold the knife out in front of me.

"Syker," I call, "come out."

Silence.

Marcus comes down the steps through the companionway behind me. "See anything?" he whispers.

"Too dark," I say. "There are four cabins beyond the galley. Two on the left. One on the right beyond the head. One all the way forward."

The confined area smells musty from all the saltwater Syker's men have bucketed out.

"Want me to go first?" he asks.

"I got it," I say. "Just cover me."

I step forward through the galley, past the dining table and row of seats. I see a glint of silver in the sink, the white countertops. I walk toward the corridor to the cabins.

Even in the near total darkness, I can see the doors are all shut. I open the first on my left. Three portholes above the waterline provide just enough light to glance around the berth.

A bed. Small desk. Chair. Cabinets.

"No one," I say.

Marcus stands in the doorway. "Try this one."

I nod. "Careful."

Marcus opens the door on the other side of the hallway. Hinges creak. "Nothing," he says.

I open the third cabin near the front of the boat. The layout is similar to the first. No one is in the room.

I check the head next. Empty.

That leaves only the berth at the forward end of the hall. I can barely see my hand in front of my face. I feel around for the doorknob. Find it. Turn. Push the door open.

This room is larger than the other three, almost certainly Syker's. I step forward into the dark, holding the knife in front of me. My heart hammers in my chest. I scan the room. A wide bed lies before me. Nightstands on either side. A skylight overhead provides just enough light with which to see.

Suddenly the door crashes into my arm. My knife clatters to the floor. I fall backward, toppling over, and Marcus tries to brace my fall. I hit the ground in the hall and then look up and see Syker standing in the doorway.

"Who do you think you are?" he demands, a sneer on his face.

Marcus kneels beside me. "Stay back," he growls.

"What have you done to my village?"

"I burned it to the ground," Marcus says, "you son of a bitch."

I get to my feet, brace myself against the wall.

Syker looks us both up and down and shakes his head as if he feels sorry for us. A stern father disappointed in two wayward sons. "You don't understand this world at all."

I stare at his dark silhouette in the doorway.

"I know why we're here," he says. "I know what happened to the world."

"Everything you say is a lie," I say.

"Truth," Syker says, "you'll find, my boy, is the greatest lie of all."

I say nothing.

"Join me." Syker reaches out his hand.

The boat pitches and rolls over the waves. I widen my feet for balance.

Aleah's voice comes from the end of the corridor near the salon, "Syker."

"My dear, sweet girl." He peers down the hall.

"Hiding in the dark?" Aleah asks.

"You haven't told him, have you?" Syker says. "You've kept it from him all this time."

She grips her spear in her right hand, and says, "Your lies won't work now."

He laughs and turns to me. "She's lied to you, boy, from the moment you first met. Tell him. Tell him, Aleah!"

"Tell me what?" I say.

"She can't love you," Syker says. "She knows far too much."

"He's lying, Jordan." Her voice cracks.

"You led him on," Syker continues. "You cracked open his poor, pathetic heart. I can see it in his eyes even now. You made him believe you loved him, and yet you haven't told him anything."

"What are you saying?" My heart thuds against my ribs. I can't breathe. I feel sick, like I might throw up right on Syker's shoes.

"She knows everything." Syker laughs again. "She's playing you, boy, and you're too naive to even see it."

I'm not sure if it's the pitch and roll of the waves or the weight of Syker's words, but my knees buckle, and I fall toward the wall. Marcus grabs me, holds me upright.

"And now it's all over," Syker says. "Her lies have caught up with her."

"Don't believe him, Jordan. Trust your heart."

"Yes, Jordan, trust your heart," Syker says, mimicking her. He shakes his head. "Listen to her. Does she love you? Really? Think about all those moments together."

"Stop it," Aleah cries.

"You are pure evil," I manage to say between gritted teeth.

"If only that were so," he replies.

In the darkness of the corridor between the cabins of the boat, I feel Marcus slip something into my hand. Cold sharp steel. A blade to drive into Syker's heart. I look up and into Marcus's eyes.

"Look out!" Aleah cries. "He's got something in his hand!"

I turn to look at her in disbelief. Then all at once, Syker emerges from the doorway, a dagger the length of his forearm in his hand. Its silver blade glints in the semi-darkness, and before I can move out of the way, Syker throws it at me. Marcus steps in front of the blade, and it strikes him in the center of the chest, propelling him back into my arms.

Before I can even cry out, Syker rushes forward, knocking Marcus and me against the wall and to the floor.

"No!" I cry.

From the floor, I see Syker face off with Aleah. I look down at Marcus.

"Hang on," I say.

"I can't breathe." Marcus gasps for air.

"Hold on," I tell him, "please." I try to lay him on the floor gently, but out of the corner of my eye I see Syker walk right up to Aleah, lean forward, and embrace her, pulling her close.

"Aleah! What are you doing?" I fall back to the floor, Marcus's body beside me.

"It's time to finish it," Syker says. "Take your spear and drive it into his heart."

She looks from Syker to me.

Marcus coughs.

"Do it," Syker says. "Kill him, and we'll finally leave here together, my love."

"Aleah!" I cry.

She steps toward me. Her spear shimmers in the half-light of the dark corridor.

"Aleah? Please."

"Do it!" Syker says. "Drive your spear through him!"

"How could you?" My voice is plaintive, barely audible to my own ears.

"I never loved you," Aleah says gazing into my eyes. "You were too foolish to ever understand what this world is really about."

"Good," Syker says.

"And your greatest mistake," Aleah says, turning to face Syker, "was trying to make me believe you!"

She drives the spear into Syker's chest. The old man's eyes widen. He gasps. She withdraws the spear with a ruthless tug, and he staggers backward toward the companionway. He clutches at his chest. Falls onto the stairs, pulls himself up the steps toward the cockpit.

In my arms, Marcus says, "Finish him." And then his eyes close.

"Marcus," I cry. "Open your eyes. Marcus! No, please no."

But it's useless. Marcus is gone.

I rise and stare down the dark corridor at Aleah and then to Syker who has reached the cockpit.

I brush past her, our eyes glancing into one another's for only an instant. Once above deck, I grab Syker and drag him toward the side of the boat. Wren is at the wheel, and I see that we have moved beyond sight of the island.

The first light of dawn is breaking on the horizon, and in every direction lies a vast and endless ocean. The sailboat plows forward over the waves, and I kneel and look into Syker's eyes.

"This is what happens to evil."

"I created order on that island," he wheezes. "I am a good person."

"You believe that?"

"It's the truth!"

I kick Syker overboard. "Tell it to the sharks."

The boat races onward to the north, and I stand and watch as Syker's arms flail in the waves.

"I don't deserve this!" he cries. *"Don't leave me!"*

Soon his voice is lost amidst the sound of the ocean beating against the side of the boat.

Aleah emerges from below deck and the look on her face says everything.

"Marcus," Wren whispers. Her face is colorless, her fingers on the wheel have gone white.

"Syker killed him." Aleah looks back toward the darkened corridor.

Wren rushes past her and down the steps. I take the wheel. Aleah stays where she is, and we both stare out over the water and listen to Wren keen, her screams like an ice pick to whatever is left of humanity.

And to the east, the sun begins to crest the horizon.

PART 3

Fifty-two

The boat carves its way northward across the open ocean. I say little, resolved to scan the horizon from the helm, hands on the wheel. Keep busy, I tell myself. Do something useful. Don't think. The wind and salty air ruffle my hair. My pants are ragged, my feet bare. Blood has dried under the tips of my fingernails.

Wren and Aleah wrap Marcus's body in a sheet. They weight it with a spare anchor and prepare the sea burial along the port gunwale. The wind flaps their shirts and blows their hair.

No one cries.

They look at one another, their eyes a language of their own. Wren kneels first, then Aleah. The body passes into the wake and sinks into the depths of the ocean, and I feel as though something vital has broken inside of me that will never be repaired.

•••

By sunset, I've secured the wheel with ropes tied to cleats atop the port and starboard gunwale. I peer at the helm compass.

Wren studies me.

"Think that's north?" She stares at the horizon ahead of us.

I nod.

For three more days and three nights, we travel onward maintaining a course with the compass and stars as our guides.

Fifty-three

On the fourth night, I am at the wheel under a cloudy sky with a steady wind whipping my hair.

I remember waking at sea, not unlike this, scared and alone, fighting for my survival. I keep thinking of Marcus who stepped in front of Syker's blade to save my life. Guilt and shame hammer my brain.

I look forward over the bow and see only darkness and whitecaps. Waves splash against the side of the boat, which rises and falls on the growing swells. Aleah emerges from the companionway. She sways a bit and walks toward me. Sits in the cockpit only a few feet away.

"Wind's picked up," she says.

Hands on the wheel, eyes on the sea before us, I say nothing.

She studies the waves and the clouds. "Why do you love me?"

What a question. I say nothing for a long while, and then, "It's foolish, isn't it?" I say, "In a world like this."

"I wish I could answer that," she says, "in a way that didn't break my heart."

•••

I wake in the midship cabin in darkness to the sound of Aleah calling for me. Something crashes to the floor in the salon, and I feel the pitch and sway of the boat on large waves. I roll over and see water on the floor in the black. It looks like a creek sloshing back and forth. I swear.

Through the porthole above my bed, lightning flashes in the darkness. Water crashes against the thick glass. My feet hit the floor, and water sloshes against my shins. When the boat pitches on the next wave, the rush of water in the corridor beyond my door is a torrent.

I stagger into the salon and see Aleah coming toward me from the open companionway.

"We're in trouble."

Another flash of lightning reveals Wren at the wheel.

"We secured the lines," Aleah says. "The sails are down."

The boat dives forward, and a wave crashes over us like a waterfall. Aleah ducks as it pours down into the companionway and salon, and I see Wren struggling to remain standing at the wheel.

"I'll get her." I pass Aleah and brace myself as I step out into the cockpit.

The boat pitches forward again, the bow diving into a wave that is higher than the length of the ship itself. The sails are down and the boom is secured, but the wooden mast is leaning aft.

"Get below deck!" I shout at Wren.

The water knocks me to the floor of the cockpit.

Wren grabs my wrist. "Hang on!"

Water floods over us, but she refuses to let go.

I look up and see Aleah emerge from the companionway. She struggles toward us. I am on my back. Wren stands over me, her hand clutching mine. The boat pitches forward again, diving down the back of another wave. We start to slide toward Aleah, and I watch in horror as the mast splinters above us.

For an instant, the massive wood hangs at an angle. Then the bow dives into the next wave, and another wall of water comes over the front of the ship. The sea strikes the mast, and it falls toward us, crashing over the wheel with spectacular force.

The mast rips through the stern, splitting the back end of the boat in half, and I am washed overboard.

I swallow the sea, coughing and gasping for air, the water so cold it takes my breath away. I panic. My muscles seize up. I fight to keep my head above water. A giant wave curls with a sound like thunder crashing down toward me. Everything is frigid darkness, roaring wind, looming waves.

And then I see her. Her outstretched hand reaching toward me, her eyes wide, her mouth moving, screaming my name. The image is seared into my mind and nothing—*no one*—will ever be able to erase it.

Fifty-four

By dawn the sea is flat. The wind is dead calm. I cling to a piece of fiberglass that has sheared from the back of the boat. The fragment is only slightly larger than my outstretched body, but I can lie flat on it. Carefully, I sit up. I gaze around the entirety of the visible ocean and see no sign of Aleah, Wren, or other remains of the boat.

I balance on my knees. I cup my hands over my mouth and call out as loudly as I can, "Aleah!"

•••

Though the sea is flat, water gently spills over the slab. I'm stretched out on my stomach, dozing in and out of consciousness. The water is cool on my skin, contrasting with the sun's heat on my back. I drift like that for most of the day.

I slide off the slab only twice, both times by intent so as to relieve myself in the sea. I have no difficulty climbing back onto it, and I see no other signs of debris until late in the afternoon.

The object I spot looks like trash. At first I try paddling from the slab. That proves too cumbersome, and so I slide into the sea for the third time, steeling myself against the fear of sharks. I swim toward the object.

A clear plastic jug sealed with a blue top. Looks like water inside. I remember seeing containers like this stored on the boat. I swim quickly back to my slab and hoist the half-filled container onto the fragment. I kneel in the center, balancing as well as I can, and open the cap to sniff the contents. I sip it. Clean drinking water to last a day or two.

I drink only enough to wet my mouth and throat, then cap it and make sure the top is tight.

I scan the rest of the ocean as far as I can see and spot nothing out of the ordinary. Just water. Endless water.

Fifty-five

The drone approaches near sunset. I hear it before I see it. Only minutes before I'd slid into the water to inspect a mass of floating plankton some distance away.

It flies straight toward me.

I swim underneath the seaweed until I find a particularly thick patch. I rise slowly toward the surface and allow just enough of my face above water in order to breathe.

The mass of plankton is thick, and I can only partially see through it. I remain silent.

The drone hovers. I watch it circle the area, scanning for other remains. After a few moments, it flies toward the mass of plankton. It inspects the area and rotors back and forth along the floating seaweed for several minutes.

It doesn't seem to see me. At its closest, it's a stone's throw away, but my entire body is below water. Only part of my face is above the surface, and that is covered in thick plankton.

The machine rises into the sky and returns to the slab. It circles a few more times, then spots the plastic jug of water, which has slid off the slab into the sea.

A mechanical arm emerges from the drone's body. The appendage has a circular blade at its tip, which cuts a big gash across the top of the jug.

Silently, I swear at it, imagining how satisfying it would be to rip it apart and watch it sink into the ocean.

The drone rises into the air with a detestable gnat-like sound: *whhrrr*. It pivots, makes one final scan, and then rises higher and takes off across the sea far away from the plankton and the slab until I can no longer see it.

I listen until I can no longer hear it and then wait a while longer. Finally, I emerge from beneath the seaweed and return to the slab. I inspect the damaged water container. I tear the top of the jug back entirely and sip what water remains inside. Spit it out. Already too much seawater. I empty it.

I scan the cloudless sky for several minutes, expecting the drone to return.

It does not.

Fifty-six

Three nights after the drone encounter, a gentle rain starts to fall, spattering down upon my bare skin. There's no wind, just the sound pattering on the slab and on the inside of the plastic jug, and it reminds me of something deep in my past, from before...before the raft and the boy and the island. Before Aleah. For some time, I don't move, just close my eyes and relish the cool water on my face and listen to it fall on the calm sea all around me.

I'm starving, hungrier than I've ever been. Eventually enough rain fills the jug that I sit up and try a few sips. The water makes me cough, but I manage to keep it down. The rain continues to fall windlessly, and the jug to captures water throughout the night.

•••

Two more days and nights adrift at sea. Even with the captured rainwater, I haven't eaten in so long I can't think clearly. I hear voices, and in some moments, I am unable to discern whether the voices are coming from some outside source or from inside my head. I start to believe that whoever who put me on the island—a deity, for all intents and purposes—may be talking to me and that it wants me to kill myself. Then I think the deity is testing me to see if I can endure its directives and that that itself is part of its assessment of me.

I mumble, my lips barely parting.

My body is deteriorating, muscles feeding on themselves to prevent organ failure, staving off collapse of the whole system. My beard is rough, my skin darker, but not burnt, in the relentless sun.

•••

A curious thing happens. As the days blur and my water runs low again, I begin to obsess about composing a message to those who may discover me after I'm dead.

Why is this important? I don't know. Why does it matter? It probably doesn't. What possible difference could it make to others to know anything about me, my experiences, my thoughts and feelings, once I'm dead? I can't answer the question, but I can't let it go, the impulse to leave something behind.

I begin to imagine a written language of symbols in my mind. I can picture them. I lie on the slab, raise my finger toward the sky. I draw what I see in my mind. The first image is the island. Next I picture the ocean and the waves. I draw three wavy lines.

Then I picture Aleah and drop my hand to my chest. I have no idea how to represent her. No symbol comes to mind. I think about it for a while, then raise my finger to the sky and draw a circle.

Maybe I'm beginning to understand my true self—the innermost essence of my being—beyond what I've been conditioned to think, feel, and be. Like the kid on the raft said, you can't know why you're here until you know who you are. The two are inseparable, light and dark, life and death. One can't exist without the other. And who we are is much, much deeper than what we've been conditioned by life to be.

I can see it in my mind like a golden energy—like an infinite source of all that is—the essence of my being. I know I'm losing my mind. Vaguely, I wonder what's the longest someone has survived at sea. I wonder how long I've been alone. I reach up and watch my finger trace Aleah once more in the sky.

O

Fifty-seven

Eyes closed. Sounds.

A bird. A sound I've not heard since leaving the island. Its cry triggers something deep in my neural network. My eyes start to twitch but do not open.

The sound of a wave. A wave lapping something. Not the sound of the open ocean. The sound of water striking an object.

Together the two sounds wake me. I'm weak. I open my eyes enough to see through my lashes. Everything is a haze. I rest from the exertion, then I see it. An object floating on the sea. I clear my throat, wipe at my eyes, try to sit up. Everything hurts.

The birds are circling above the object. I squint into the distance. It's a piece of wood. From a boat? There's a body on it.

"Aleah." A surge of energy courses through me and my vision clears.

She lies face down, the wood rising and falling on gentle swells. I slide off into the water and swim to her, pulling the slab with me.

Damn the sharks.

"Aleah!"

She doesn't respond. Doesn't move. I near her floating raft, raise my hand, and touch her face. Her skin is warm. Alive. I tread water and watch her. She doesn't wake, and I pull myself up onto her raft and hold my ear to her mouth.

Her breathing is labored and rattly, her lips are swollen and cracked, caked with dried blood. She is emaciated, her eyes sunken in their sockets. There's dried blood around her nose. I rinse her face with seawater. Her eyelids flutter.

"Aleah."

She opens her eyes, tries to focus.

"*Water.*" It's barely a whisper.

"Hang on."

I pull my slab closer, drag one end onto the end of her raft so mine won't float away, and then inspect the plastic jug of rainwater. There's not much left. "Can you drink?"

She doesn't respond. I gently roll her over and hold the jug to her mouth, tipping it slightly. She swallows.

"More."

I tilt the jug toward her lips and can see her throat move.

I pull it away, watching to see if she can hold the water down when she closes her eyes and mouths, "Thank you."

Her eyes are unfocused, but she seems to recognize me. And for a moment, I think I see the corners of her mouth quirk up in a small smile.

Fifty-eight

She dozes on and off, and each time she wakes, I give her a few more sips of water. All around us, the sea stretches in every direction, and a gentle breeze pushes us on the current. I stare out at a line of clouds hovering on the horizon.

I feel her touch on my leg and turn to look at her. "You look much better." She hasn't been able to sit up yet, but her eyes can focus and, after another sip, she finds her voice.

"You saved my life, Jordan." She glances at the jug. "I would've died."

I point to the clouds in the distance. "Perhaps we'll get another rain."

Her eyes, sunken and shadowed on her too-thin face, smile at my hope. "If we don't," she says, "if I don't survive—"

"Stop talking like that. We've got this now."

She doesn't look at me, and we're silent for a long time.

Finally, I ask, "Wren?"

She frowns and shakes her head.

•••

Overnight, the line of clouds descends over us as a sea fog. The air cools. The wind picks up, and the sea swells grow choppy. She abandons her piece of wood and joins me on my larger slab.

"So cold," she says.

"Hold me close. It'll keep us warm."

We huddle together on the slab as water spills over its sides on the larger swells. We keep sliding and must adjust our position. Neither of us sleeps.

By daybreak, the fog is so thick I can't see more than a few yards in any direction. The breeze remains steady and pushes us deeper into the cloudy haze. I hold Aleah, and our bodies shiver against each other.

Fifty-nine

The sound of the ocean breakers reaches me through the fog. I'm sitting up, and Aleah lies with her head in my lap. I stroke her wet hair, thick and heavy with salt.

"Is that...?" she says.

I point. The fog is so thick I can't see much, but through the haze, as if through a curtain, a beach appears. The land beyond the beach slopes steeply uphill, but whatever resides higher up is enveloped in clouds.

I look at the empty jug.

"Swim for it?"

She nods.

I slide off the slab into the water. My body stings from the immersion. She joins me, and we swim toward the breakers and beach. The waves are large now, and I have no way to know whether the seabed is sand or rocks. I try to help her stay with me, but a swell lifts and pushes us forward, curling and breaking as it roars toward land. I lose sight of her.

"You got it?" I call.

Then, I see her, her head still above water. She slowly treads toward the beach. I look back and can no longer see the slab. Another swell picks us up and catches us in its rip curl, and we both tumble underwater. I strike the ground a moment later, a rocky ocean floor. I brace myself with my hands and feet, then stand in water up to my chest. The rocks dig into my soles.

I don't see her. "Aleah!"

Another crashing wave rolls toward me, its power nearly knocking me down. I stumble but remain upright. Then I see her rise from the water, standing on her feet on the rocky ground. She struggles out of the water and up onto the beach. I stagger to her, as she falls into my arms. She shivers uncontrollably, and I help her walk up the beach toward the cliffs that rise into the thick fog, shrouding and clinging to everything.

"F-f-freezing." Her teeth chatter, and we hold one another and drop to our knees in the sand. She looks toward the sea and the massive rocks that rise above the surface like giant fingers. Exhausted, we settle back into each other's arms and listen to the waves.

170

Sixty

It's still foggy when we set out along the shoreline, but it's not far before we come to a narrow canyon carved by a creek that's cut a channel in the beach on its way to the sea. We drop to our knees to drink, then head inland, following the creekbed. We are weak beyond reckoning, and the climb up the canyon is difficult. The plants along the creek are overgrown, and we stop often. The water is cold, and we use our hands to cup it to drink, then to wash the salt off our skin.

I point out insects: flies, then beetles. She sees the first bird, a swallow that shoots from a shrub. As we climb farther up the canyon, towering redwoods rise above us. The creek widens in spots and trickles downhill in small waterfalls. The stones along the creek are large, smooth, and dark. Moss grows on exposed parts, and soon we are enveloped in a hillside coastal forest.

The narrow bridge we come to is the first sign of civilization. It has been built for foot traffic across the creek. I stare at it for a while, then scan the forest for other signs of people. An overgrown path leads away on either side. Tree branches, pine straw, leaves, and plants cover the bridge. The undergirding is made of steel, but the boards across the bridge are rotted and old. Enough remain, though, to support crossing.

"Which way?"

"This way." She picks up a stick and begins clearing her way along the path.

Sixty-one

The house is a dark brown clapboard perched on the hillside. The fog is too thick for me to see the ocean from here, but I can hear the roar of the surf through the mist coming up the cliffs.

The windows are broken, and plants have reclaimed the area around it. Several pine trees have broken through the deck, pushing rotted boards up and away. Some are twice my height. The roof is covered in plant debris, and a fallen redwood limb has ripped a hole in one side.

"Careful." I peer in through a shattered window. Jagged pieces of glass lie beneath the sill. Something skitters across the floor in what had been the kitchen. Mist creeps through the treetops.

We circle the house and discover a gravel driveway that leads away from the property.

Aleah says, "Might be food."

The front door is locked, so I use a rock to clear a window. We climb inside. The hole in the roof from the redwood limb has left a pile of debris on one side of the living room. Rainwater has rotted away the floorboards underneath it. Shattered windows in the kitchen provide entry for wildlife. I spot rodent droppings on the floor.

And yet, in other ways, the house is strangely intact. A kitchen table and chairs remain together, as though someone recently finished breakfast. A lone coffee mug stands atop one of four placemats, the liquid inside long ago evaporated, leaving a brown stain at the bottom.

Aleah finds dishes in a cabinet near the kitchen sink, tries turning on the faucet. No water.

I open a pantry door. "Look at this."

Shelves on either side hold cans of food, boxes, jars, and containers. The canned food appears well stored, and the pantry itself has been shut and is dry and dark.

"See anything we can use to open this?" I hold a can of potatoes and look it over closely for any signs of swelling or cracks.

•••

I set about building a fire in the fireplace using wood from a pile outside the home. It's damp, but I find matches in a tin on the mantel and newspapers in a drawer beneath a firewood rack next to the hearth.

Before tearing up and wadding the top paper to burn, I look at the photos on the front page. I freeze, my heart lurches.

I glance across the living room and see Aleah focused on the pantry. For a reason I can't quite understand, I don't want her to see what I've found. Instinctively, I turn my back so that if she were to look in my direction, my body would block the papers from her sight.

Then I look down at the front page and see the ruins of a large city. The photo has been captured from an aerial vantage point high above the devastation. Maybe taken by a drone?

Another photo shows people herded together in fenced cages inside a building. Everyone wears air-tight helmets and ventilators. I study an inset close-up of a woman who holds a child to her chest. The girl and her mother both wear helmets with ventilators and clear face shields.

"How's it going over there?" Aleah asks.

I crumple up the page and place it beneath the wood in the fireplace. "Found matches."

From inside the pantry, she says, "There's enough food in here to last us weeks."

I strike a match, hold it to the paper, and watch it ignite. I close the drawer beneath the firewood rack, hiding the remaining newspapers. The flames curl past the image of the city ruins, past the woman and child with helmets and ventilators inside a fenced cage. The wood catches, crackles, and pops.

"Yeah, I, uh, think we could stay here for a while," I say, "with the canned food. Water from the creek."

"Everything okay?" She looks at me by the fireplace.

"I just hope this chimney is intact." I make it look like I'm checking the flue. "Seems to be pulling the smoke well."

"Well, I don't feel strong enough yet to go far," she says. "I just want to rest, recover."

Sixty-two

Nourished by food cooked over the fire, I find blankets in a closet in the bedroom. I drape them over Aleah and myself, and we lie together on the sofa, watch the fire, hold each other. Outside, the night is cool, the mist hangs like a curtain in the coastal forest beyond the shattered windows, and the hole in the roof opens onto the sound of a light breeze rustling the trees. I glance at the shut drawer that holds the newspapers beneath the firewood rack.

"What if knowing your past life made you unable to continue living this life?" she asks, suddenly.

"I'd still want to know."

"Why not just embrace *now?*" she says. "Why do we need to know what lies beyond anything other than this moment? I want to be completely present, feel your body close to mine, with gratitude in my heart that I'm still alive."

I stare at the fire. I grow sleepy and think maybe she is dozing. In the quiet, I ask, "Don't you want to know who did this to you?"

She says nothing for so long I think she's fallen asleep. Then, "I'm not sure it matters."

"Help me understand."

"What am I going to do, spend the rest of my life seeking revenge? I've wasted far too much energy and far too much time filled with anger at what others have done to me. I don't want to spend the rest of my life filled with bitterness or resentment, filled with shame or rage."

"How do you let it go?"

She pulls me close. "You focus on the good in the world, Jordan. Focus on the good."

•••

I wake while it is still dark outside. I add wood to the embers in the fireplace and find clothes in the bedroom in a chest of drawers. They're not a perfect fit, but they're better than my rags. In a closet near the front door of the cabin, I find coats and boots. The boots are a size too large, so I go back into the bedroom and find thick socks. Better. Still too large, but I lace them nonetheless. They feel heavy and awkward on my feet.

I unlock the front door and step outside. Everything is wet. The fog has not lifted. I can scarcely see the driveway. I glance back through the window and see the flames coming to life in the fireplace and Aleah still sleeping on the sofa.

I walk away from the house toward the driveway. My boots crunch on the gravel, note the weeds are as high as my chest.

I find the next home soon, set back in the woods from the drive, abandoned as well. I continue hiking up the gravel drive. I walk for a while and count eight homes before I come to a paved road.

Two yellow lines mark the center, and I can't see far in either direction because of the fog. The pavement is broken in places and weeds grow among the cracks. I listen to the still of the night.

I return home. She's still asleep. I remove my coat and boots, then add more wood to the fire and poke at the embers.

Quietly, I pull out the drawer beneath the firewood rack, afraid of what else I will find. In the glow of the firelight, I remove the newspapers, set them on the floor, and begin to skim the images. In one picture, I see a line of cars that stretches for miles. People walk beside the vehicles, which are stranded on the highway. Everyone wears masks with face shields and ventilators.

Aleah shifts but doesn't wake. Her face is peaceful.

The image on the front page of the fourth paper in the stack stuns me. She wears an airtight helmet with the ubiquitous clear face shield and ventilator. Her hands are cuffed behind her back, and a phalanx of police officers escorts her down the steps in front of a building, amidst a teeming mass of people.

The mob is enraged and, by her expression in the image, she looks terrified of the crowd. Some carry signs. Faces are frozen in the act of shouting. Fists are raised in anger.

Inset within the column of words, I see a smaller photograph of me and a sailing crew standing on a large racing vessel at port. We hoist a large wooden plaque above our heads, jubilant and victorious.

I stare at the pictures for a long time. I look over at her asleep on the sofa. Then I put the newspaper on top of the blazing logs in the fireplace. I watch as the image curls and burns. I skim the rest of the papers, see nothing else that has meaning for me. I put them all atop the fire.

Under the blanket on the sofa, Aleah stirs. She mumbles, "Where did you go?"

"To the blacktop at the end of the gravel drive," I say.

I watch the blaze and feel her watching me. Soon she closes her eyes and drifts back to sleep.

Sixty-three

Two days later, I find the rifle in a house three properties from the paved road. A bolt action .22 that holds one round at a time. A box of shells lies on the shelf above the rifle, and it looks like only a few have been removed.

I withdraw one and hold it in my palm. Aleah watches me. We exit the home, a walnut-colored two-story log cabin, and I step down off the porch and work the bolt.

"You know how to use that?" she asks.

"Simple enough." I slide the shell into the chamber and lock it into place with the bolt lever. I raise the rifle, pull the safety back, and then sight down the barrel. Aiming toward a stump, I rest my finger on the trigger for a moment, then pull. The kick of the stock against my shoulder is familiar, almost reassuring, and a spray of wood explodes from the stump. The crack of the gunshot echoes in the stark silence of the forest.

...

We stay among the enclave of houses for so many days I lose track of time. There are no signs of anyone else around, and the evidence—the height of the trees that have broken through the deck, the state of rusted porch swings, patio tables, a riding mower covered in plant growth—suggest no one has lived in the area for a long time.

One car remains in the enclave, a fallen tree resting across its shattered front window and crushed hood.

Searching the houses, we find enough supplies to last us a while. Backpacks and sleeping bags, a tent, canteens, clothes, coats, and boots that fit better than the ones I first tried.

•••

The highway sign has been wrenched backward as if by a gale-force wind. It clings to a single wooden post. Around us, the forest looms, trees stretching toward the sky. I stare at the sign and listen to the sound of a woodpecker needling the bark of a tree nearby in search of insects.

"What do you make of it?" I ask.

Aleah shakes her head.

I lower my backpack and prop my rifle against it. The sign itself is green, the letters spaced in a noticeable pattern. Most are bunched on the left side of the sign in three rows. Substantial space separates the writing on the left from the smaller set of symbols on the right.

I try to lift the sign to straighten the metal, but it's too thick. I pick up a stick and trace it over the symbols on the top left:

Lucia

Aleah slips off her backpack and puts it on the ground. She removes her canteen and takes a sip. Caps it. Only seems vaguely interested in the sign.

"You mind if I carry that for a while?" She nods toward the rifle.

"What do you think this line means?" I point with my stick.

Los Angeles   310

She picks up the rifle, raises it, tries the bolt lever, and then sights the barrel down the double yellow line of the road.

"What does it mean?" She pulls the trigger and listens as it dry clicks. "I think it means the world is gone."

Sixty-four

We pitch our tent on a bluff overlooking the ocean and an enormous arch bridge that spans a wide, deep canyon. The two-lane expanse is made of concrete, and since the fog has lifted, the sun dapples the blue sea in brilliant flashes of light.

Aleah builds a fire, and we cook rice and a large can of beef stew and eat until full. Then crawl into the tent and lie back on the sleeping bag, keeping the flap open.

My mind is spinning. I can't escape the images from the newspaper—Aleah in handcuffs, Aleah surrounded by an angry mob—and as the days wear on, I become more and more convinced I'll never be able to tell her what I've seen and that I was foolish for pushing her to leave the island, foolish for insisting we should try to learn about our past lives. And, most of all, foolish for thinking we should try to find answers to the question of who sent us to the island and why.

Her head rests against my chest, and I run my fingers through her hair as a gentle breeze rustles the tent flap.

"I wonder what happened to everyone on the island after we left," she says. "What if we're the last two people on Earth?"

"I'd be happy with that."

She places her hand over my heart and turns to kiss me. "It scares me," she says. "This kind of loneliness."

I relish the warmth of her body against mine. I trace the outline of her ear and whisper, "Then hold me close and don't ever let go."

•••

It's late in the afternoon, the sun hanging above the western horizon, when we reach the coastal city two weeks later. After a full day of hiking, we stop and stare in silence. From our vantage point on a rise above the city, we take in the homes and abandoned cars spread out before us. The lack of movement is like a blow to the chest, and at my side, my fingers flex and tighten on the cold metal of the rifle barrel. Below us, in the distance, a bay empties into the ocean through a deep channel, like a sentinel guarding a graveyard.

The houses are built close to one another all up and down the hill descending to the bay. As we walk down the middle of the street, my eyes dart from one side to the other, from window to window, blood pounding in my ears, my body alert to movement of any kind. A bird flies across the street in front of us, and I whip the rifle up to my shoulder before I know what I'm doing.

I lower the rifle and rest trembling fingers at the small of Aleah's back as she peers into the window of a car parked at the side of the street. "We could spend the rest of our lives going from house to house."

I swallow, my nerves still on edge. "And maybe never find a single human being."

Sixty-five

The lodge is on the waterfront along the main street, its glass door shattered. Signs of looting are everywhere. Broken shop windows. Shelves overturned. Debris strewn across floors. A door to a restaurant kicked in and lying on the ground. I stand inside a small shop, the floor covered in rubble. I pick up a child's toy amidst the remains. I hold the rifle in one hand and the toy in the other, staring at it, trying to imagine a world I can't remember.

"It's almost too much to process."

Aleah, outside on the sidewalk, beckons to me through the window.

"Come on," she says.

•••

The storm rolls in across the bay just after sundown. Lightning splinters over dark water illuminating the room where I stand mesmerized by the view. A moment later, a peal of thunder rattles the cracked window, and Aleah looks up from tending the fire in the small fireplace. The smell of smoke masks a musty odor in the room no doubt caused by rodents, rain, and years of disuse. To provide cross ventilation for the fire, we've propped the door to the covered walkway open with a chair.

In my peripheral vision, I see movement, and when I turn from the window and look across the motel room, a child stands just outside the doorway. She's dressed in filthy rags, her face is covered in dirt and grime, and her feet are bare. Her hair is soaked and stringy. She glances from the fire to the rifle propped against the chair beside me. On her hip, she wears a knife in a sheath that is practically as long as her thigh.

Before I can get the words "Hey wait" out of my mouth, she darts away.

Aleah turns from the fire. "What?"

"Girl." I grab the rifle, step outside, and peer down the covered walkway in the direction she went. Rain pools in potholes in the parking lot and pours off the roof. It is pitch-black outside, save for the dance of firelight coming from our room and the occasional flash of lightning. I hear the clatter of an overturned bottle on concrete from an alley.

"Jordan, don't!" Aleah grabs my arm, but I wrench free and head toward the end of the walkway. A bolt of lightning brightens an empty alley. I turn back and see Aleah standing outside our room in the glow from the flickering fire. One more glance at the shops across the street, but I see nothing. The rain is falling in sheets, and I see no sign of movement. The girl is gone.

I return to the room. "Did you see her?"

"Just a glance."

"I think I scared her when she saw the rifle."

Aleah starts packing her things. "We need to go."

"Right now?"

"She can't have survived by herself," she says. "And if she leads others back to us, I don't want to be pinned down in a room with only one exit."

•••

After we pack up and refill our canteens with rainwater, we set out along the dark shoreline, walking beside the shadowed wrecks of abandoned boats scattered on the beach like skeletons. Thankful for the clothes, boots, rain gear, and tent we found while scavenging, we're protected from the worst of the storm. We set up camp on the beach, take turns keeping watch, and head out again at daybreak. Eventually the road ends, and we find a footpath leading up from the beach into the hills. We continue up the trail, hiking higher into the hills until we can hear but no longer see the waves below. A stiff breeze comes in from the sea, bringing a cold mist. We've seen no sign of any other human since leaving town.

Sixty-six

By morning, the fog has lifted. The hillside is treeless, grassy shrubland, and far down the slope, at least an hour's hike away, lies the ocean. The wind is strong, and I carry the rifle to a bluff on the far end of the clearing.

To the south, as far as I can see, houses cover the hills and valleys. The sheer number of them, like grains of sand on a beach or leaves in a forest, takes my breath away. What happened here? Where is everyone? Why can't I remember?

•••

We hike down to a coastal highway and walk along it for two more days. I imagine watching us from high above, two tiny dots like ants crawling among the ruins of a lost civilization. It's overwhelming. I couldn't have pictured so many houses if I'd tried. We pass from one town to the next and onto the next. Words fail us. What is there to say when confronted with the enormity of it all? The loss. The emptiness of abandoned shops, storefronts, homes, apartments, motels, buildings upon buildings upon buildings. Roadways, exits, on-ramps, cars, trucks, side streets. Silence surrounds us. Except for the sounds of our shoes on pavement and our own breathing and an occasional bird, everything is quiet.

•••

On the fifth day after our encounter with the girl, we enter a deserted seaside town. The beach is carved like a giant crescent around a cove. Waves come toward the shore and turn to roaring breakers. Disused houses and buildings line the coast.

A wooden pier built on concrete pilings extends out over the water at the cove's midmost point. I walk across the gray sand to a stairwell. Barnacles cover the pilings.

A shop is on the beachside end, and I place my backpack on the ground outside its shattered doors. Glancing up, I catch my reflection in a broken piece of glass wedged in the doorframe. I hardly recognize myself: long hair, beard, dirty face, heavy overcoat, too-large jeans, and blue eyes so intense I have trouble holding my own gaze.

"You okay?" Aleah asks me.

"Yeah," I say. But the question echoes through me. How can I be "okay" if I don't recognize who I am? If I don't recognize myself. I step away from the ghost of the man I see in the broken glass and study the pier's length. At its end, it forks into two shorter extensions.

Aleah enters the shop and rummages around until she finds a few bottles of water. Like most of the places we've seen, the store has been ransacked. Debris is everywhere. She hands one of the bottles to me. I take a sip and then refill my canteen.

I find a push broom in a back closet and make a space for us inside the shop, setting up the tent to keep insects away. But as evening falls, I find it stuffy and too warm, so when I'm certain Aleah is asleep, I grab the rifle, quietly unzip the flap, and step into the open air.

Just outside the shop, there's a wooden bench, and I sit and listen to the surf. I'm not sure why we should go on. During my time on the island, I'd imagined that our escape and discovery of the mainland would give us some insight into the meaning of our lives. I'd been certain it would help me to make sense of why, after everything, I'm still alive, who'd taken our memories from us and for what purpose. I have a driving need to understand what it all means, but finding this ghost of a civilization, I'm more confused than when I'd been on the island. Thoughts weigh on me until I can hardly breathe. What is left for me? For us? Does my life have no other purpose than to wander from place to place until I eventually die?

I listen to the sound of my breathing and the sound of the surf and bring them into harmony. Inhaling and exhaling with the crash of waves rolling up the beach while imagining a world deserted. Eventually, I doze off and dream I'm walking toward the end of the pier. Something keeps pulling me toward the sea. It feels like the wind. There is no sound. I picture myself going over the edge, falling into the water, and then I hit the surface and discover I can walk on the water. I begin walking toward the horizon only to realize I'm slowly sinking. My shoes are covered, then my ankles, then the waves are lapping at my shins and knees, and then I hear her calling my name. Aleah. On the beach, waving for me to return. Waving. Come back, she calls. Come back!

Sixty-seven

Something catches my attention in the depths of sleep, and I startle awake, disoriented. The sound of the surf is familiar, but there's something else... A mechanical sound in the distance, coming toward me, getting louder.

I shake my head, stand, and stretch, and that's when I see it: lights from a vehicle rolling slowly toward the beach through the abandoned streets of the seaside town. The girl we encountered more than a week ago darts across the street, and I automatically reach for the rifle.

The sky to the east is just beginning to brighten with the first light of dawn, but the beach and pier are still dark. I creep toward a corner by the shattered doorway and kneel in the shadows.

The vehicle looks like a white caterpillar with large black windows along its sides. It is flexible, bending around corners. Lights are positioned around the roof. I can see the girl illuminated briefly in a darkened store entrance. She crouches, waiting.

"Aleah!" I whisper.

The vehicle stops on the street not far from the end of the pier. I pat my coat pocket to make certain I have the box of ammunition. I finger one of the shells and slide it into the chamber, locking the .22's lever and pulling back the safety.

A door near the front of the vehicle opens, and a ramp extends onto the ground. At first I can only see bright lights from inside, but then a figure appears in the doorway. It steps down from the vehicle and out onto the sand where the beach meets the sidewalk. The figure wears a yellow rubber suit topped with a helmet and headlamp. The visor over its face is tinted. The figure stands on the street, looking around. After a moment, another figure emerges. Similar height to the first. Similar yellow rubber suit.

"You got her signal?" Its voice sounds like it's being filtered through a machine.

"Aleah!" I whisper through the shattered doorway. "Wake up!"

"What is it?"

"Quiet. Someone's here."

The second figure says, "You hear something?"

"Sensor's picking up two lifeforms on the pier."

A third figure steps down the vehicle's ramp. I see her contours in the form-fitting yellow suit. She says, "Scared of the dark?"

A fourth and then fifth figure emerge, each carrying equipment, all wearing similar yellow head-to-foot suits with helmets and lights.

"Ricker's picking up lifeforms," someone says.

"Could be two of the children down on the beach like last time."

They gather around Ricker's sensor, which is small enough to hold in his hand. "There's no code for them," the woman says.

"What? How is that possible?"

"Look at the reading."

Aleah steps through the broken shop window and crouches beside me. "What do we do?" she whispers.

I peer around the corner and see that the girl is gone from the darkened alcove of the store entrance near the vehicle.

"There's another! She's on the move!" the woman calls out, and three figures take off running toward the beach.

"Look!" one of the yellow suits yells. "There she is! Quick! Get her!"

I stare in horror as they catch up to the girl. One pauses, takes aim, and fires a net from a long gun that unfolds over the girl, tripping her. She flails her arms and falls to the sand, screaming wildly.

The suited figures surround the girl as she struggles. "Take it easy! We're not going to hurt you."

A fourth catches up to the group. "Careful, she might bite." He looks at his hand-held. "Chip reader says it's 'Child 1-4-7-7.' Released less than a month ago near Morro Bay."

Ricker, the fifth member, points his handheld toward the pier and moves toward the group on the beach, which has started dragging the screaming girl up toward the street. "The two on the pier," he says, "surround them before they escape!"

I look into Aleah's eyes and whisper, "They've got us penned in."

She sighs and nods. With her by my side, I rise and step out into the open, walking toward the stairwell. I aim the rifle at Ricker.

The group stops and stares even as the girl continues to struggle inside the net.

"What the—?" one yellow suit says.

We slowly go down the stairwell and cross the sand toward the group. I still can't see their faces. Their face shields are tinted black.

"Put the gun down," Ricker says.

The one in the form-fitting yellow suit steps forward. "My name is Dr. Megan Ibori. We're research scientists."

"How are they breathing?" one of the yellow suits says.

With one finger still on the trigger, barrel aimed at Ricker, I slide my other hand into my coat pocket and finger another shell from the box.

"Please," Dr. Ibori says.

"Look out," one of the yellow suits shouts. "The girl's got a knife!"

The girl slashes through the netting and catches one of the scientists' suits in the leg. A mechanical voice from the man's helmet booms out, "Contaminant! Contaminant! Suit breached! Contaminant!"

He swears and falls to one knee. His hands come up to his throat. "Can't breathe!"

"Maxwell!" Dr. Ibori shouts.

One of the other yellow suits shoots something at the girl. It strikes her. She convulses and ceases moving.

Aleah lunges at the man, and he turns and shoots her in the chest. Her entire body seizes, and she collapses onto the sand.

I fire my rifle, striking the yellow suit who shot the girl and Aleah. The bullet strikes him in the shoulder, and the man whips back, dropping his device.

"Contaminant! Contaminant! Suit breached!" The scientist falls to the ground and begins to writhe, clutching at the neck of his suit and choking out, "Can't breathe!"

I reload while staring at Dr. Ibori.

"Wait!" She throws up her hands. "Don't shoot! Please!"

I close in on her, aiming the rifle at her heart. Ricker backs toward the street. "It's just a stun gun!" Dr. Ibori says. Her hands are up, palms toward me, and she's speaking in a voice that is clearly trying to calm me down. "They're not hurt. They'll both be okay in just a few minutes."

The one who the girl hit with her knife lies on the sand and is not moving. The one I shot still writhes but is no longer speaking. Soon, he stops moving altogether.

"He shot them!" I'm in no mood to be placated.

"It's a stun gun, an electrical charge!" Dr. Ibori says. "They'll both be fine."

The girl moans and starts to move her hands and legs.

I glance around the group and then focus on Dr. Ibori. "Who are you?"

"I told you. We're scientists. Put the gun down. Please!"

I take a step closer and lift the barrel of the rifle so I'm aiming at her black faceplate. I'm no more than four paces from her. Ricker is now on the ramp up to the vehicle, and the third scientist is inside the door. I can see a small chamber, large enough for three people to fit into if standing close. The scientist inside the chamber slowly lifts his hand toward a red lever. "What's he doing?" I say, "Put your hand down!"

"Don't shoot!" Dr. Ibori says. "We mean you no harm!"

She backs toward the vehicle. Ricker steps into the chamber beside the other scientist. Dr. Ibori reaches the ramp. She holds her gloved hands up, palms facing me.

I hold the rifle ready to fire again. On the sand, Aleah groans.

Dr. Ibori steps into the chamber inside the vehicle and says, "Seal the door and gas them!"

The chamber closes in the blink of an eye. I fire. The bullet strikes the metal door, ricocheting with a spark. Then I hear a hissing sound issue from valves opening along the roofline.

Everything slows. The rifle suddenly weighs as much as a tree limb. I feel like I'm moving through deep water. My legs buckle. I drop to one knee on the sand and reach out my hand toward Aleah as dark spots dance before my eyes.

Sixty-eight

When I wake, I am strapped in a seated position in the back of the moving caterpillar. My arms, torso, and ankles are bound. Aleah and the girl are unconscious, strapped into seats similar to mine, and all three of us are in a sealed compartment in the back of the vehicle.

"Aleah?" I whisper.

She doesn't respond.

The two bodies from the beach lie in sealed and transparent containers. They're still wearing their yellow suits, but their helmets have been removed. The other three scientists sit across from the containers, and they've also removed their helmets. Two men and one woman.

One of the men has pale skin and is bald. The other man has dark straight hair. The woman is dark-skinned with short hair. She sits on a bench and stares out the window at the passing landscape of abandoned homes and buildings.

The vehicle drives itself.

One of the men, the bald one, comes to the window of the compartment. I look into his expressionless eyes. His face tells me nothing, but I sense sadness in the vacuum of his stare.

He presses a button on his side of the window and says, "My name's Ricker."

I say nothing. The woman wipes tears as she stares out the side of the vehicle from her bench.

"The one you shot," Ricker says. He glances over his shoulder at the woman. "Was like a son to her."

"I'm sorry. I just hit him in the shoulder. It shouldn't have killed him."

"That's not what killed him."

"Then what?" I ask. "How do you die instantly from a gunshot wound to the shoulder?"

Ricker shakes his head and looks at me with sorrow and pity, the depths of which I can't begin to comprehend. "I'm sorry," I say again. "What was his name?"

"Andrews," Ricker says. "Kaden Andrews. Student of hers."

I look from Ricker to Dr. Ibori, who continues to stare out the side of the vehicle at the passing landscape.

"Why did you trap the girl like she was some sort of animal? She was screaming. Scared. She's just a kid."

Ricker stares at me for a while. Finally, he says, "You really don't know?"

"What don't I know?" I can hardly breathe. These people may have answers to my questions, but I don't even know what my questions are any longer. "Why are you wearing those suits? What's wrong with you?"

Ricker gazes at me through the sealed compartment. He frowns, then nods slowly. He opens his mouth to speak but then turns to Dr. Ibori.

"Save it," Dr. Ibori says, continuing to stare out the side of the vehicle. "He'll find out soon enough."

Sixty-nine

A disembodied voice announces: "Exiting Hollywood Freeway."

I glance from Aleah and the girl to the scientists in the forward compartment. Dr. Ibori and Ricker stand as the vehicle weaves through abandoned cars. The third scientist—Ricker says his name is Takamura—lies on a bunk staring up at the ceiling. Since we left the beach, I've gazed out the windows at the endless homes, billboards, bridges, overpasses, and neighborhoods through which we've passed. Nowhere have I seen a living human being outside of the vehicle. Finally, we come to a stop before a giant gate. The voice says: "Anag. Norisis, Inc. Compound. Vehicle processing. New lifeforms detected."

Dr. Ibori glances at us and then turns back to say something toward the front of the vehicle. I can't hear her inside the sealed compartment, but she points toward us. I look at Aleah and the girl. They're awake now, but none of us can move in our secured seats.

"Scanning," the voice says.

Dr. Ibori says something else in response, and she looks at me.

"Proceed with new lifeforms to Sanitation Unit Entrance 107."

"What's going on?" I ask. None of the scientists respond to me, and I can't tell whether they've even heard me.

The gate opens. "Entering Anag. Norisis."

"What's going on?" I shout. "What is a sanitation unit? Where are you taking us?"

I watch helplessly as the vehicle climbs into the hills on a curvy two-lane road. As we ascend, I glimpse the ruins of a vast city. At one point, I spot the remains of a skyline. The buildings look as though a massive force has blown away their westward-facing sides, leaving exposed beams and wires.

"Look at those craters," I say. "What happened here?"

Beside me, Aleah is silent.

Inside the craters, nothing remains other than brown exposed earth. All structures near the rims are obliterated, and the blast radii extend out a good distance. The craters are uniform throughout the city. The scale of the destruction is enormous, although much of the valley outside the blast radii appears intact.

"Approaching sub-Los Angeles entry," the female voice says, "Sanitation Unit 107."

I struggle in my wrist restraints. The young girl—Child 1-4-7-7—watches me. "Human," she says.

I shout at the scientists, "What're you doing to us?"

They appear not to hear me, and the caterpillar-like vehicle approaches a tunnel carved into the side of the hill. The entrance is sealed with heavy reinforced steel.

"Scanning vehicle," the disembodied voice says. "Proceed to Sanitation Unit 107 docking."

The tunnel doors slide open. The vehicle continues forward, and the doors shut behind us.

Seventy

The tunnel is scarcely wider than the vehicle, and it spirals down as we descend underground. Exterior lights along the roof brighten the drab concrete walls, and soon we enter a wider docking area and roll to a stop.

Liquid and foam spray over the exterior of the vehicle from nozzles in the ceiling, walls, and floor. The windows are covered, blurring the view. Then a bright reddish light envelopes us, and the three scientists in the forward section stand. Next, violet lights on overhead tracks fill the cavern. They make three passes, and the windows dry and are covered with a thin film. Blowers blast something from the wall on the right, then rotate over the vehicle. The windows clear. A flexible tunnel emerges from a doorway and attaches to the vehicle. The three scientists step into the chamber and then exit into the tube.

•••

The room is white, and the air smells like freshly crushed almonds. The floors are smooth, hard, and cold against my bare feet. A stainless-steel table stands before us. Aleah sits in a chair that matches my own. They took the girl away some time ago.

The door to the room has no knob. The ceiling is made of white concrete and is supported by four beams. In the center a large round showerhead hangs, and I spot a small speaker.

A feminine voice speaks: "Please remove your clothes. The doctor will be in soon."

I look at Aleah.

I ask the ceiling, "Where did you take the girl?"

"There is no need for alarm," the voice says.

"Can we see someone, please?" Aleah asks.

The voice says, "We must sanitize you first."

"What does that mean? 'Sanitize' us?" I ask.

"We'll make sure you're clean. It's a safety precaution. No need for alarm."

Everything about this is disturbing, but something about bare rooms with showers for sanitizing people makes my skin prickle. I stare at Aleah.

"Please," the voice says, "the nurse will be in to take your clothes and provide you with a gown."

Aleah starts to undress. I sigh and join her, removing my coat and shirt. I use the chair to balance as I take off my jeans.

"Please place the clothing on the table," the voice says.

I bend down and pick up the pile from the floor and do as asked.

"Chair's cold," Aleah says.

The door opens. A figure in a protective yellow suit enters. I can see nothing through the dark faceplate on the helmet. "Are you the nurse?"

The figure removes the clothes from the table, places them in a bag, and seals it shut.

"They said you'd give us a gown," Aleah says.

The figure says nothing and exits the room with the bag containing our clothes. The door seals shut once more.

"The nurse forgot the gown," I say to the ceiling.

"Please step toward the center of the room beneath the shower-head."

"Why should I listen to you? Why should we do what you ask? What is this all about?"

"You must be sanitized," the voice says.

I glance from Aleah to my own filthy body. My hands are blackened with grime. My beard is nearly down to my chest. I cross to the door. The doorframe looks airtight.

"Please step away from the door," the voice says.

I try pushing. It doesn't budge. I see no way to open it from inside the room.

"Do not touch the door, sir, or we will call security."

I feel a sting of shame and embarrassment. The feeling of being watched yet not being able to see who is watching me fills me with anxiety. It must be affecting Aleah similarly because she says, "Could you just step toward the middle of the room like she asked?"

"No," I say, fighting through my feelings of helplessness and confusion. "If I want to stand over here, if I want to touch the door, I'll do it."

"Sir, if you touch the door once more," the voice says, "we will call security."

"Jordan, please." Aleah stands naked beneath the showerhead in the ceiling.

I look down at my own naked body as rage surges through me like a tidal wave. I pound on the door.

"We're calling security," the voice says. "Sir, step away from the door now."

I want to hide, but where? There's nowhere to go. We're trapped. Naked and powerless. I can't protect Aleah. I can't protect myself. I can't... I realize I'm about to spiral out of control and shame and anxiety begin to swamp my senses. I realize Aleah is embarrassed, too, but her unease is with me for not complying with the commands.

"What?" I say.

"You're going to get us into trouble."

"I think we're already there."

"She told you not to touch the door," Aleah says, impatience coloring her voice. "She said she was going to call security. Why would you do it? Why would you touch the door?"

The urge to pound on the door is overwhelming. I start to walk toward the door again.

Aleah reaches out and grabs my arm. "Don't."

The voice in the ceiling says, "Security has been notified."

"Jordan, please."

I don't touch the door.

"Please step toward the middle of the room," the voice says. "Security is watching you."

"This is messed up." I step toward the middle of the room once again.

"Good, now stand perfectly still."

I look up at the showerhead. A hissing sound like steam begins to issue from the fixture, but there's no water. This is not a shower.

"What is that?" I demand. "What are you doing?"

The gas fills the room, and I see dark spots and grow light-headed. Aleah's eyes close, and she sways toward me. I brace her, as we both go down to the cold, white concrete floor.

My muscles fail as the gas seeps into my lungs and then into my bloodstream. I look at Aleah who is already unconscious on the floor beside me. I summon all my strength, reach out my hand, and caress her cheek with my fingertips.

PART 4

The Clear

I can no longer feel my body, and the only semblance of conscious awareness I perceive is the light. I am surrounded by it, a kind of golden white energy. I hear nothing, smell nothing, taste nothing, feel nothing, and the only thing I can distinguish is the light. I feel no emotion, positive or negative. No anxiety or fear. I simply am there, in the light.

Day 1

"He's coming 'round," the voice says.

"Vitals?" another voice.

"110 over 68," the first voice says. "Pulse is steady at 58."

"How you feeling?"

"Sick."

"We have a pan here," the first voice says. "Just turn your head."

"That's right," the second voice says. "This way."

I open my eyes and see a bright light over me. An arm reaches toward my face from behind the light. I feel the crinkle of paper underneath my body, a loose cloth is draped over my loins. A stainless-steel pan lies beside my head. I roll over and vomit into it. I feel a cool, damp cloth wiping the side of my face. I close my eyes.

"Too bright," I say.

"You're going to be alright," the first voice says, feminine and caring.

"Have you seen the results of the patch test?" the second voice asks.

"Yeah."

"My name is Jordan," I say.

"Just try and take it easy," the first voice says.

I open my eyes. Her face leans to the side of the light. Soft lean features. Eyes the color of the desert. Thin brown eyebrows. Lips curved in a slight smile but showing no teeth. Her hair is brown with streaks of silver in it, pulled back in a ponytail.

"Where am I?"

"You're in an exam room." She dabs the cool cloth on my forehead.

"Where is Aleah?"

The two women glance at one another. The woman with eyes like the desert says, "She's right here beside you."

I turn and see her on a bed adjacent to my own. She's not awake.

I try to raise my hand to shield my eyes from the light, but my arms are shackled to metal rails on the side of the bed. A padded sleeve grips my bicep, and my skin is as clean as I've ever seen it. No signs of dirt.

"What's this?"

"Blood pressure, heart rate. You appear to be making a full recovery."

"Where's the girl?"

The other nurse leans forward and scans my forehead. "Hold still," she says. "We need to take your temperature."

"Why am I—" I see Aleah is shackled as well. "Why are we locked to the beds?"

The second nurse has auburn-colored hair and green eyes. She is tense. She has freckles on her forearms.

"Ninety-seven point eight," she says over her shoulder. Then to me, "What do you remember?"

"We were on an island," I say. "With no memory of our past lives."

"An island," the nurse with green eyes says.

"People were watching us," I say. "No one could remember life before. Some kind of experiment."

"You believe you were in an experiment," she says.

"We managed to escape," I say, "on a boat. But a storm destroyed it. We were adrift for days."

The nurse makes a note on a tablet. She nods, appearing to accept my explanation.

I ask, "Where is this place?"

"Just rest now," she says.

"What is Anag. Norisis, Inc.?" I ask. "What is sub-Los Angeles?"

The nurses exchange a look I can't interpret.

"Where did you hear that?" Desert Eyes asks.

"On the vehicle that brought us here. What is this place?"

"Sir, please try and stay calm."

"I would be calm if someone would answer my questions. Why am I shackled to the bed?" My metal cuffs clank against the bars.

I gather from the look that they exchange that something unpleasant is coming.

"Darvodan," Desert Eyes says.

"One twenty-five?"

The first nurse nods, and the other hands her something.

"What is that?" I yank my arms hard enough to bend the bars toward me. "Why're you doing this to us?"

She places something cool on the side of my head near my temple, a kind of adhesive patch.

"You just need to rest."

"I. Feel...better. Now."

Day 5

I wear a paper medical gown and sit on a stainless-steel chair in front of a stainless-steel table, the metal cold against my skin. A group of researchers—all young men, all in lab coats—sit around the table studying me. They look as calm and reasonable as a jury. A rectangular mirror is embedded in one wall. I look at it and don't recognize myself.

They've shaved my head and beard. My skin is clean. The dirt under my fingernails is gone. I recognize my eyes, but otherwise I'd think I was looking at a different person.

One researcher opens a wooden box on the table. Another holds a tablet.

I have wires taped to my head, and my left index finger is clipped with a plastic caliper. All wires connect to a machine adjacent to the table. My bicep is secured with a blood pressure cuff.

One says, "We're trying to help you." Several of the young men nod.

I look at the group, from one set of eyes to another, and I feel resistance falter in my mind.

Even as I sit there battered, drugged, taped, and monitored, I suspect they've chosen a large group like this with intention.

"You want compliance," I say.

"You've been through a great deal, and we care about you," one says. The young men really do seem to care, but I can't figure out why. Is it all an act?

"Where is Aleah?"

"We need you to focus on you. We want to help you get better."

"You put me on the island," I say. "You did this. Why?"

Several of the men shake their heads. I feel shame gnawing at me, as though my resistance is repulsive to them. The will to comply grows like a brush fire among dry grass.

"You've suffered through enough. You can put it all behind you, if you want."

"Then let me go," I say. "Let us go."

"Please just know that we care about you. All of us. We accept you. Unconditionally. And we want you to feel better."

"Yes," another says, "we're here to help you."

"What do you mean you accept me unconditionally?"

"It means we care about you, just as you are, and we want to help you regain your strength and mental faculties."

"Who is that girl? Child 1-4-7-7?" I ask.

One of the men takes off his glasses and places them on the table, rubs his eyes, and then looks up at me. His lips are turned in a slight frown, but his eyes are calm and nonjudgmental. He folds his arms in front of him and leans forward. I'm close enough to see that he has glacial blue eyes.

"We're not giving up on you," the man says. "The treatments are beginning to work. You're getting stronger. Your vitals are good."

"Why do I need treatments? What are they for? Did you put me on the island?" The man looks right into my eyes and shakes his head, and I know he's lying.

"No," he says. "We did not put you on the island."

"If you didn't, you know who did. And you know why."

Another of the young men at the table sighs. Silence fills the room. I feel the weight of the group, the social pressure of their performance of caring for me and of trying to help. The first man says, "We accept you and care about you. No matter what. We want to ease your pain and suffering. The isolation. The trauma. The loneliness."

Another says, "Despite everything, no one should have to go through what you've been through."

The other men shoot him a dark glance, and silence fills the room. I focus on him. "Despite everything. What does that mean? And if you didn't put me on the island, who did?"

The lead researcher shakes his head calmly. His eyes are full of compassion and concern, as if he really cares about my well-being.

I fight not to lose control, to keep my voice even like theirs. "You all keep saying that, but it's not helping me. Answers to my questions would help. Letting me see Aleah would help. Letting me go would help. But for some reason, you're keeping me locked away in a cell where I haven't seen sunlight for what feels like a week. You won't let me see Aleah, and you won't answer basic questions. Like who is that girl? Why did those men trap her like an animal? Why did they die when their suits were breached? Where did all the people go? What the hell happened to the world?"

The lead researcher nods sagely, as if he understands my frustration—which makes me more frustrated. "In time," he says. "You'll get your answers in time."

I almost believe him. "What have you done with Aleah?"

The lead researcher ignores the question and turns to look at the other young man beside him with the box.

"In time, Jordan, we would like to restore your memory."

I huff out a laugh. "You want to fry my brain again."

"We know how hard this must be on you, and we don't want to make things worse. Recovering your memories will be distressing. We can give you more time and rest if you need it."

"'Rest'? Locked in a windowless cell for another week? That's not rest. It's torture. What do you want from me?"

"We would like to help restore your mental functioning."

"I think my mental functioning is just fine."

"You have no memory."

"I have no memory from before the island."

"We can help you with that."

"Who put me on the island?" I demand.

"That's what we'd like to help you recall."

"You want me to play along with this charade?"

"There's no charade."

"If you didn't do it, who did?" I struggle to keep the anger out of my voice. "And why did you erase my memory, why did you erase my ability to read and make sense of the world? Why would you do that? You give me answers and maybe I'll cooperate."

"You'll get all your answers when your memory is restored."

"And what about Aleah? You going to restore her memory, too?"

"Aleah is undergoing her own treatment. You'll be reunited soon. But first, we have to make sure you're ready. We care—"

"Yes, I know. You care about me." I let out a long, frustrated sigh. It really does seem like these men care, but there's something in their manner that feels rehearsed, as if they've said similar things to countless others for years and years and know their methodology will work on me, too. In time.

In the days that follow, their routine is the same. Every session they grill me with questions or present me with various mental tests. Then they medicate and monitor me in my windowless cell.

Day after day after day until it all starts to blur into one general feeling of emptiness, loss, and alienation created by the questions and the tests and the men in lab coats, and I find myself losing the ability to distinguish one session from another that happened the day before or several days before.

Day 27

"Why are you looking at me like that?" I ask. Something seems different today. They look tense, anticipatory perhaps.

The group is once again assembled around the table, all eyes on me as if I'm an animal they're training in a lab. The leader motions at another among the group who presses a button on the table. The lights in the room dim, and a projected image appears on the blank white wall opposite us.

"This," the leader says, "was taken from the vehicle the morning our team discovered you and the young woman on the beach."

The video displays a figure running across the beach in predawn darkness. Lights from the vehicle's exterior reveal the girl running across the sand. The team in yellow suits traps her in the net, and then I watch as my own figure and Aleah's come onto the screen. They drag the girl, and she screams wildly at them. I see the rifle in my hands.

The man pauses the video on one clip that clearly shows the scene. "You want to know why we're holding you here," the lead researcher says, "watch."

"I know what happened," I say. "I don't need you to replay my nightmares over and over."

"The girl strikes Maxwell with her knife. Maxwell's suit is breached. He falls to the ground. Aleah attempts to intervene and is subdued. Then you open fire on Kaden Andrews, effectively killing him."

The researchers play the video.

"I thought they'd killed the girl," I say. "I thought they'd killed Aleah. These 'scientists' acted aggressively, right from the start. It was dark, they're wearing suits and helmets, and we couldn't see their faces. It was self-defense."

"So you admit you were mistaken?"

"Mistaken? I don't admit a goddamn thing! I was doing the best I could with the information I had. If you're going to fault me for self-defense and for trying to protect someone I love, I think you need to take a long hard look at yourselves to consider who's to blame. Who started the confrontation? Who trapped a child like an animal? Who shot her and Aleah, electrical charge or no? It wasn't me, that's for sure. I was trying to protect them!"

One of the men curses. Another leans back and blows out a long breath, shaking his head in exasperation.

"Please, Jordan," the lead researcher says, "you've been deeply traumatized." Well, I can't argue with that. "We want to help you."

"Stop saying that! For god's sake, why can't you just answer a few simple questions? If you want to help me so much, why are you keeping me here, locked in a windowless cell for what feels like a month? Tell me who I am and why I was sent to that island and what you want with me now. You people are going to drive me crazy!"

"We want to show you. We do. We want to help you understand, but it is—"

"Then stop all this nonsense and tell me! All you've done is make me doubt myself, doubt my integrity, doubt my intentions. And you call this helping?"

"Before we give you the answers you so desperately want, we need to determine if you're so traumatized that you're dangerous."

"Dangerous?" I look down at my hands and think about what happened on the island, think about the boy in the raft, think about Syker and Marcus and Wren and Aleah. Always Aleah. I shake my head in wonder at what I've become. "If you think I'm dangerous now, just imagine what I'll become if you don't tell me the truth, now that I know that you know and aren't telling me."

The lead researcher motions for the other to bring the lights back up and to kill the projected image on the wall. "Enough."

Day 30

A voice in the ceiling says, "Remove your clothes and place them in the bin by the door."

I rise from the bench at the stainless-steel table in the center of my cell, walk to the door, untie the gown, and drop it in the bin.

"Return to the center."

I do so and stand naked, waiting. I've given up protesting these demeaning intrusions. Easier just to go along.

The lock clicks, and the door opens. A female researcher about my age enters the room wearing a white lab coat and carrying a tablet about the size of a clipboard. With brown hair pulled back in a ponytail, she's wearing semitransparent prophylactic gloves and glasses, which she pushes up on her nose as she looks me over.

She cocks her head, studying me. "How're you feeling today?" She comes closer. Her eyes are dark brown with flecks of gray around the edges. I say nothing. I stand like a statue and stare at a spot on the wall. She walks slowly around me. She writes on her tablet.

"Open." I do, and she shines a light inside my mouth. "That's fine."

I feel her rubber glove touch my neck. She looks at her wristwatch. She places the tablet on the table.

"Follow my finger." She shines the light in my eyes and slowly moves her digit back and forth, up and down in front of my face.

"Do you miss your partner?" she asks.

"Of course," I say.

"Good." She feels my genitals, lifts them, inspects them. My arousal is reflex. I stare at the spot on the wall while she continues. I say nothing.

"We need to know if you can reproduce." She removes a specimen cup from her lab coat, opens it, and then lubricates her hand with petroleum jelly and begins to stroke me. "Good," she says in a soft voice. "Like that, yes, that's right. Whenever you're ready."

When I'm done, she puts a cap on the container. Seals it with medical tape. Slides it into the pocket of her lab coat. She returns to the metal bin by the door and removes her gloves. Drops them on top of the gown.

"Do you know if you're capable of..." She pauses, searching for the right word. "...breeding?"

I stare at the spot on the wall. "Don't you have video evidence of that?" I say, "From the island."

"I need you to look at me, Jordan."

I turn toward her.

She says, "You are special. Very special."

"Is she okay?"

"Almost fully recovered."

"You've taken care of her?"

"Our team has given her great attention."

"When will I see her?"

"Did you? On the island?" She clears her throat.

"I'm capable of having sex, if that's what you're asking. Didn't I just prove that?"

"Very well then." She pats her lab coat pocket. "We'll check your sperm count."

I stare at the researcher. A strand of brown hair comes loose from her ponytail and falls down her face as she makes a note on the tablet. She looks up at me and strokes it back behind her ear, then pushes her glasses up on her nose and half-smiles at me.

"I just want to know she's alright."

The young woman picks up the metal bin, and the door opens. She glances back at me as she exits.

"May I have another gown?" I ask. "Please?"

"After you shower."

The door seals shut behind her.

Day 38

They lead me down a hallway. Everything is gray concrete: the walls, floor, the ceiling. I smell something like burnt oil and cooking grease, but after weeks underground isolated in a windowless cell, I'm no longer entirely certain of my senses. We stop at a non-descript door, and one of the young men punches a keypad. The sound of the mechanical lock clicks, and the door opens with a weighted hiss.

A figure sits on a stainless-steel bench at a steel table. She wears a medical gown, its back gaping open between the drawstrings. Her head is shaved, and her back is to me. She doesn't turn to see who is entering her cell. She stares straight ahead at the wall opposite the door.

I draw in a sharp breath. "What have you done to her?"

At the sound of my voice, she moves her head but does not turn to see me.

"Jordan, we care so much about you," the researcher says, and I tell myself not to explode.

"Is she alright?" I force the words out, modulating my voice.

"You both have made great progress. Would you like to speak to her?"

I look from the researcher to Aleah who has scarcely moved.

"Yes," I say.

The researcher motions for me to enter the cell. I look at several of the other young men in lab coats, standing around, watching me. They all seem happy for me. Several nod their heads, encouraging me. One smiles.

I step into the room, feel the cold hard concrete on my bare feet, the draft at the back of my gown. I notice the large rectangular mirror embedded in the wall to my right. I see her toilet. The open shower and drain in the corner. Two small metal bunks with thin foam pads for mattresses form a right angle in the forward left corner of the room.

The door seals shut behind me.

A strange feeling overtakes me. I know they're watching through the mirror. I know at any moment they might enter the room and separate me from Aleah if I say something they find displeasing. I know in essence that everything I might say, everything I might do is unnatural, a performance molded and shaped by the power they hold over us and the one-way stare of the mirror. The feeling is so unnerving, my disassociation so complete, that I question the compassion stirring in my chest, the rush of love I feel for Aleah.

"It's me," I say.

She still doesn't turn to look at me and I walk slowly around the room to see her face. She glances up at me, and then averts her gaze and stares at a spot on the table. I study her, and shame wells up in my chest. A complicated shame because I feel responsible for us being kept here like lab rats. And I am acutely aware of every behavior and action, every physical movement of my body, every gesture, every word, and the implication of each precise moment's meaning to those watching me.

"I love you," I say. "If nothing else, please remember that."

She looks up at me and smiles.

"How are you?" I ask.

"Fine. How are you?"

I glance at the mirror and see myself standing at the table, head shaved, my medical gown partially opened at the back between drawstrings, my legs and feet bare, the medication patch on my left temple.

"I feel good," I say. "I've missed you."

She gestures like a hostess entertaining a guest. "Will you have a seat?"

Tears sting my eyes, an intense emotional reaction to her question, and I promptly quell it for fear of how it might be interpreted by those watching.

I sit at the table. Aleah's hands are folded in her lap.

If I ever want these researchers to grant me more freedom, I have to comply. I took the lives of Maxwell and Andrews. That they're allowing me to live is a kind of grace. They could've killed me on the spot, and that would've been a perfectly acceptable response.

"They want to restore my memory," I say.

"I know," she says.

"From before the island."

"They want to know if we can reproduce," she says.

I see a slight smile rise at the corners of her lips, a flicker in her eyes, a suggestion of the way I'd known her in those moments on the island when I was certain she was most alive and free.

"I'm sorry I made you leave," I say.

"You didn't make me leave."

We look at one another for a long time.

"They've forced my hand," she says. "You'll never love me again. Of that, I'm certain."

"I don't understand."

She glances at the mirror, then looks deep into my eyes. I shiver. "No matter what happens," she says, "I want you to know I love you. When I first saw you on the island, I wasn't sure what to think, but I fell in love with you, Jordan. Just as you are."

"Truly?"

"They removed my birth control and boosted my fertility to make it possible to reproduce. I'm grateful."

"And that's what you want?" I ask. "With me?"

A glance at the mirror. "Yes, of course," she says, looking deeply into my eyes.

•••

They leave us together for three days. We know they're watching us and, in a strange way, it makes it more pleasurable. It's a performance for them, even though it means so much more to us. To finally have human contact, to finally be able to touch and hold each other. To sleep with her in my arms means more than I can put into words. We use the shower, the metal cots with thin foam pads, the table and chairs, the floor, against the walls, against the one-way mirror.

Three times they remove her from the room for several hours and then return her after an examination.

Day 44

When the door to our cell opens, I look up and see two scientists in lab coats enter the room. I glance at Aleah. One is Dr. Ibori, whom I've not seen since she left the vehicle with Ricker and Takamura on our first day underground. The other scientist I don't recognize.

"My name is Markwart," the man says. "I believe you've met Dr. Ibori. How're you feeling today?"

Neither Aleah nor I respond.

"May we?" Dr. Ibori motions toward the bench at the table.

Markwart glances at Dr. Ibori, then meets Aleah's stare. "We're done with our preliminary testing," he says, "and treatment."

I study the man's face. He has short-cropped brown hair and pale skin. His eyes are the color of a storm cloud.

"You've now been with us for over six weeks," Markwart says. "It's not lost on us what this experience must be like for you."

I glance at the mirror embedded in the wall. "Others are watching?"

"Of course," Markwart says.

"Why're you keeping us here? What's this all about?"

"You've both described this island you were on," Markwart says. "For years, in your case, Aleah."

I glance at her. "Yes," she says.

"Who am I?" I ask. "Am I... Am I human?"

Markwart exchanges a glance with Dr. Ibori. "You're much more than that, Jordan. Much more. But your question is of the utmost importance to us. At what point do we become posthuman? An artificial heart, bioengineered skeletal resilience, respiratory advances or immune functioning, or are we human distinctly because of our brains... what then when we enhance neuron activity, cognitive functioning, creativity, or restore memories that may change civilization forever?"

Dr. Ibori says, "We'd like to offer you and Aleah an option."

"What option?"

Markwart removes a clear sealed canister from the pocket of his lab coat. He places it on the table in front of me. I see a liquid inside the container. It could be water, though it appears more viscous. The lid is transparent.

Markwart says, "We'd like to restore your memories."

"From before the island?" I ask.

"Yes," Dr. Ibori says.

Aleah shakes her head. "No." The word is whispered, but we all hear it. Agitated, her eyes dart back and forth between me and the scientists.

"It's important to understand the decision must be yours." Markwart removes a second canister from his lab coat and places it on the table next to the first. The second canister contains a dark black liquid of similar viscosity.

Dr. Ibori says, "When you drink the Clear—"

"Please," Aleah interrupts. "Don't do this to him."

"Aleah," Markwart cautions, his brow drawing together.

"When you drink the Clear," Dr. Ibori says once again, "your memory from before the island will be restored."

"I knew it would come to this," Aleah says. "I knew you would do this."

"Perhaps additional treatment," Markwart says to Aleah, "would help to clear your mind of its turmoil."

I picture the newspaper images I saw in the cabin of Aleah under arrest, angry people yelling at her, the faded photos I set ablaze in the fireplace.

"And the other?" I ask.

"We call this 'the Night'," Dr. Ibori says. "Take just a shot of the Night, and the memories from before the island will forever be beyond your reach. Your desire to know about your previous life will ease. You'll be at peace."

"The memories are beyond my reach right now, and I don't feel at peace," I say and pick up the clear canister, holding it up to the light.

"That's because they're buried in your subconscious, still acting on you but without your conscious awareness of them. The Night erases those memories forever from your subconscious."

"What about my ability to read?"

"By drinking the Clear, the glucose metabolism within your default mode network will be chemically restored so that you'll be able to access your memories, including those of the Broca's area that will enable you to visualize and decode written words. You'll be able to read again, Jordan, and at a speed like no other 'human' ever could."

"Why in God's name are you doing this to us?" Aleah asks. "You're going to destroy everything we've worked so hard to rebuild."

"Aleah," Markwart says, "Jordan wants to know who he is. He needs this."

"No, he doesn't. It will destroy him."

"We've come so far with your treatment," Markwart says. "Please be calm. Or we'll separate you again."

Dr. Ibori speaks up. "Aleah, it's all he ever wanted to know since waking at sea. Who he is. Why he's here. Who put him on the island."

Aleah's eyes are pleading. "You don't want to do this, Jordan. Please."

"What do you mean it will destroy me?"

"You don't want to know," she says. "Trust me."

"The Clear works like so many chemical alterations of the brain," Dr. Ibori goes on. "Your recovered memories will not only include those from before the island but also residual artifacts that may seem to come from previous lives encoded in your DNA and passed from generation to generation."

"So it's hallucinogenic?"

"No," Markwart says, "the memories will be completely real to you."

Dr. Ibori adds, "And they'll be useful for the rest of your life."

"It's not an alteration," Markwart says. "The value is in the productive use of the memories you'll then have. It may be better to think of it as restoring the mind of someone with Alzheimer's."

I stare at the two canisters, my eyes darting from the Clear to the Night. "So you're testing whether we want to know the content of our past lives," I say, "or to be free of the anxiety of never truly understanding why we're here?"

"This is not a test, Jordan," Aleah says. "Don't you understand? They're going to scramble your brain even more than it already is."

"Aleah," Dr. Ibori says. "Control yourself."

"You're bastards," she spits out. "All of you!"

Dr. Ibori manifests calm and says, "This is no test."

"It's not even a choice," Aleah says. "Not for him. You haven't given him a choice in anything. It's punishment. A life sentence. You make us believe it's a choice. You make us believe we have free will. But you've rigged this from the start."

"The decision is real, Aleah, and you know it." Markwart looks from Dr. Ibori to me and Aleah. "And it's yours to make. Even if you choose to believe you have no choice, that's still a choice. That's a decision."

"Please, Jordan." Aleah reaches out to grasp my hand. "Trust me. The forgotten past is best left forgotten. No one wants to know the content of their past lives."

"No one?" Dr. Ibori asks.

Aleah looks into Dr. Ibori's eyes. "Would you want to know everything about your past lives?"

"This isn't about me, is it?" Dr. Ibori says and turns to me. "It's about you."

The Room

My heart pounds as Dr. Ibori and Markwart lead us to the room, heels clicking on the concrete floor, air filled with the smell of ammonia.

"Here we are," Dr. Ibori says, arriving at the door. There's a placard above a fingerprint scanner with markings on it. "Room 101."

Markwart presses his thumb to the scanner, and the door slides open. We enter.

A figure stands in the room with her back to us. I can't see her face. To her right, a young child stares at the wall opposite the door. A giant floor-to-ceiling and wall-to-wall video displays a tropical beach, sugar-white sand, and a lagoon's turquoise water.

"Doctor," Markwart says.

The figure doesn't turn to face us, but the girl beside her does. It is the child. 1-4-7-7.

The figure says, "You can leave us, my child. I'll see you after."

Dr. Ibori glances at Markwart, who takes the girl's hand. She walks past me and looks into my eyes with a calm, knowing expression. The door opens and then seals shut behind them.

"You have exceeded my expectations," the woman says, staring at the giant video image. "You've exceeded all of our expectations."

She turns. It's the woman from the chrome suitcase video who convinced me to leave the island. She is dressed in a blue and white form-fitting jacket with a zipper on the front. Her hair is clipped short, and her eyes remind me of a forest, shades of dark green and brown. "My name is Perí," she says. "Perí Peteia."

"Dr. Perí Peteia," Aleah says with barely disguised enmity.

"Aleah?" I say. "You know her?"

Dr. Peteia taps her lapel, and the video behind her vanishes and reveals a white wall. The two women look at me.

"You may want to have a seat." Dr. Peteia motions toward a sleek sofa.

"I'll stand." I search the forest of her eyes.

"Very well," Dr. Peteia says. "For your entire existence you've wanted to know who you are and why you're here."

"Hasn't he suffered enough?" Aleah's eyes are pleading.

"He must know."

"No," Aleah says. "This is just going to torment him."

"That's not what this is. It's up to him to decide what happens next. He must choose his destiny."

"I'll not save this mission again."

Save what? I look at Aleah but say nothing.

Dr. Peteia turns to me. "Your thirst for self-knowledge has brought you to this moment, Jordan. Your insight is nearly complete."

I say, "I'm listening."

"Aleah has tried to quiet the storm inside you, but you keep persisting. Only this time we were certain you were dead. Lost at sea. And that you'd finally taken her with you."

"I thought I *was* going to die," Aleah says. "I thought we both were."

Dr. Peteia asks me, "Do you have any idea of how much pain you've caused her?"

I swallow and hold Aleah's gaze. "I want to understand."

"We'll see." Dr. Peteia taps her lapel once more, and the wall screen behind her comes to life.

A news reporter wearing a full-body suit and helmet stands in front of a clinic. The reporter says, "He has been described as the most polarizing person on Earth. To some, he is a visionary entrepreneur whose artificial intelligence was on course to reverse the catastrophic climate change that threatens our survival. To others, he is the devil incarnate."

I see my smiling inset image in the video adjacent to the reporter. "This can't be real."

"Once hailed as a savior, Jordan DeLuna now stands culpable of destruction on a scale never before seen in human history."

Dr. Peteia pauses the video, which fills one entire wall. In the video, I wear a rubberized suit with a helmet. My hands are bound behind me, and I am being pushed into a police vehicle in front of a clinic. Everyone in the still frame wears similar protective suits. Their faces are contorted with rage, fists raised, frozen mid-shaking.

"You wanted to know about your life before the island," Dr. Peteia says. "You wanted to know who you are."

"I know my heart."

"Do you?"

"More than ever."

"And what does your heart say about the fact that the artificial intelligence your lab created unleashed the fastest-spreading, deadliest plague in history, wiping out 99.9 percent of the human population."

My jaw clinches as I hiss, "That's. Not. Possible."

"Millions of people defended you. They believed in your good intentions. They believed that the A.I. you created could reverse decades of human-caused climate change," Dr. Peteia says. "Not that it matters to them now. They're all dead."

"I would never have done that."

She ignores this. "And now the only human beings who can survive on Earth's surface must be bioengineered using the same godforsaken A.I. you developed, the same A.I. that created the plague that nearly caused our extinction."

STACEY COCHRAN

"But the craters," I say. "The city was bombed."

"Oh, that was your fault as well," Dr. Peteia says. "You see, your A.I. determined humans were the singular problem to life on Earth, and so it tried to eliminate us using every means available while sparing all other forms of life with surgical precision."

Aleah opens her mouth to say something, but then she looks away, refusing to meet my eyes.

"You see, Jordan," Dr. Peteia continues, "your A.I. chewed through all the data available, used machine learning, visualization, and computational analysis, and scaled it all up to encompass global systems and then you know what it found?" She didn't wait for an answer. "It found that humans were the cause of climate change and that the only logical way to reverse the destruction to our planet was to eliminate the problem. Your A.I. targeted biologically unique markers in the human genome that cause rapid asphyxiation in human hosts within seconds of contact. In under twenty-four hours, billions were dead."

I feel the muscles protecting my heart begin to twitch as panic arises from deep inside of my mind.

"What I have been invested in these past five years, why Aleah agreed to my predecessor's decision that she be the first posthuman on the island—"

I interrupt. "You kept this from me?"

Aleah says nothing, and Dr. Peteia ignores me. "The reason she agreed to be the first posthuman sent to the island is that we're trying to create a new world out of the destruction you and your technology unleashed on us all. We're trying to create a new species capable of surviving on the Earth's surface once more, and the great twist of fate is that we've been forced to use the same artificial intelligence you developed that nearly caused our extinction."

"That's why you didn't kill me. You knew this all along?"

"You were trying to build a better human being, acceptable to your A.I.," Dr. Peteia says. "But your experiments killed far more

228

people than you were willing to admit. Quite painfully, I might add. The pressure of it all—the shame you felt—led you to—"

"No," I choke out. "No."

"Yes, Jordan, I was there," Aleah interrupts. "The grief was more than anyone could endure. I saw you jump."

"What have I done?" I rake my hands through my hair.

"You threw yourself to your death. She, too, was forced to bear the responsibility for your mistakes, for your arrogance. You were partners. In love. And authorities arrested you both."

"But...I... No." I stammer, struggling to put what I feel into words. "I feel it. I've felt it...all this time, the weight of regret and sorrow. It's been a part of me for as long as I can remember but I never understood where it came from. It's as though I was carrying the mistakes of another lifetime in my soul."

"You claimed to love her, but your actions killed her entire family. You killed her mother and father. Her brother."

I can barely see for the blur of tears, but I seek Aleah's face, her beloved, familiar face. "God no, please. Tell me it's not true. Tell me—"

Dr. Peteia is relentless. "She trusted you with her heart, and you brought misery and shame upon her that no one could endure."

"Enough!" Aleah says. "You have no idea what I endured nor could you ever even fathom what I felt in my heart. You have no right to speak for me."

Dr. Peteia raises a skeptical brow. "Why don't you continue the story then?"

Aleah turns to me. "My family was among the first to volunteer in the posthuman experiments. But when they died, the weight was too great for you to bear and you tried to end your life, taking with you the knowledge that might've actually helped to save us. What hurt the most, though, is that you abandoned me. It was selfish. I'd lost everyone, Jordan, and you left me. Alone."

I struggle to look her in the eye, but when my gaze meets hers, I don't see blame or recrimination. I see compassion and love, and it nearly cleaves me in two.

"But you didn't die," Aleah says.

"I remember."

"That's absurd," Dr. Peteia scoffs. "You can't remember."

"I was paralyzed." The memories start to take shape in my mind like pieces of a puzzle.

Dr. Peteia looks at Aleah. "You told him?"

Aleah shakes her head. "No."

Dr. Peteia stares at me. "How could you know this?"

"You rebuilt me," I say. "You gave me this skin, these bones. You altered my brain."

"Your insight is quite clear, Jordan."

"Am I even the same person? Am I human?"

"None of us are human anymore, nor will we ever be again," Dr. Peteia says. "We're something altogether different. A new species. Posthuman."

"I'm ready to work," I say. "I'll do whatever it takes."

Dr. Peteia looks at me with calm, steady eyes. "There was a man before me who wanted to give you another chance, rescued you from the prison where you'd been left to die, paralyzed as you were. He thought it would be better to create anew with a clean slate, memories erased. Guilt gone. And so, yes, I rebuilt you under his orders. Multiple times. None of which survived on the surface until Version 3.2."

"Where is your predecessor now?" I ask.

Dr. Peteia stares deep into my eyes. "He is no more."

"The video...," I say. "You tried to warn me. He was going to kill us all. You wanted to stop him."

"As I said," Dr. Peteia looks calmly into my eyes, "he is no more."

"What do you want from me?"

"First, we must restore your memory if we're to have any hope of completing the work you'd begun."

"Why did Markwart tell us we have a choice?"

"Only Aleah will have that choice," Dr. Peteia says. "She's earned that right."

"What right?" I ask.

"To forget you forever."

I have no words.

Dr. Peteia continues, "You see, Aleah had to remember you the entire time she was on that island. She had to endure in silence the memory and pain of your failures and pretend to love you."

I face Aleah. "Is it true?"

She looks devastated. "If I'd told you, they would've killed me."

I ask, "So you're giving her the choice to live with the memories of the suffering I caused or to forget me forever?"

"You can choose to see it that way."

"It isn't really a choice, is it?"

"I saw the person you became on the island," Aleah says. "With your past erased, the essence of who you are emerged. The man I'd once known, who cared deeply for the lives of others. The man I fell in love with."

I hold her gaze. "How can you love a man who did what I did?"

"I can never forget what happened before the island. Don't you understand?"

"But the others had their memories erased, too."

"As the first bioengineered version capable of surviving above ground, knowing what I knew, I was not given that choice. Oh, how many times I wish I could've forgotten my past. I didn't want you to suffer, Jordan. No matter what happened in the past, you didn't deserve to have to live with it in the present. I didn't want that for you."

"And so you kept the truth from me?"

"I wanted to protect you. Wouldn't you do the same? If the situation was reversed, would you tell me? Would you want me to suffer for the mistakes of the past?"

"No." The photograph of Aleah in the newspaper that I burned in the cabin blazes in my mind.

"Aleah had no knowledge of the work that began following her arrival on the island," Dr. Peteia says. "Almost all who came after her were wiped clean 'like newborn children,' my predecessor liked to say."

"That's why you stopped him," I say.

"He believed he could improve the survival rate. He believed human conflict was the result of trauma and memory, but he was wrong. And we were all witnessing the social injustices, the misogyny, and brutality arising on the island. And so he was preparing to begin anew. I saved your life, Jordan, though you may not appreciate nor understand that at the moment."

"How do I make right the mistakes I've made?"

Dr. Peteia taps her lapel. The tropical beach I'd seen earlier comes to life on the wall behind her. A second shot reveals a building on a forested hillside overlooking the sea. Hundreds of drones crawl over and fly around it. The structure is made of glass and steel and consists of two geodesic domes and a tower that rises above the forest treetops.

"We are nearly finished building a new lab," she says, "above ground. With your memories restored, you must go back to work. You must advance the technology that can rehabilitate our place on Earth."

I study the images on the floor-to-ceiling display. I look at Aleah, then at Dr. Peteia. "Why would you do this? Why would you trust me?"

Dr. Peteia nods, and the muscles of her face relax. "Because, Jordan," she says. "I've come to realize something that the A.I. couldn't."

"Which is?"

"That each of us deserves a second chance. Each of us deserves the chance to learn from our mistakes and right our wrongs. Each of us deserves a measure of compassion."

I study her. I glance at the video, the geodesic domes, the tower. "Will I work alone?"

"You'll have workerbots," Dr. Peteia says. "And you'll have one assistant."

"Who?"

"Our finest researcher," she says, "who has survived the bioengineering that allows you to breathe on Earth. You're going to need the help."

I nod, considering everything she's told me, considering her motives...and her measure of compassion.

"And so you killed him, the man who sent us to the island, your predecessor?" I look hard into the forest of Dr. Peteia's eyes and see the truth.

The Decision

A glass window in the center of the cell separates me from Aleah. I am at a table pushed against it, and she sits opposite me on the other side. A silver tray with two small glasses stands before her: one with the Clear, the other with the Night.

A similar tray rests on the table before me, but there is only one small glass.

"Whenever you're ready, Jordan," Dr. Peteia says through a speaker in the ceiling.

"Can you hear me?" I ask Aleah.

Dr. Peteia says, "The window is soundproof."

I look into Aleah's eyes, and memories flash through my brain. Waking at sea. The boy lunging at me with the knife, then later dying in my arms. The first time I saw Aleah on the rocky outcropping. The creek where she put her knife to my throat. The boat. Making love by the fire in the cave. Her saving me from Syker. Marcus stepping in front of Syker's dagger to save my life. Wren and Aleah lost at sea. Finding her on the floating debris when all hope was lost.

I want to believe that she loves me. I want to believe that I can right the mistakes I've made. I want to hold her and love her no matter what decision she makes.

I reach my hand toward the window, looking into her eyes. My fingertips touch the cold, hard surface. She sits stone-still, not responding to my gesture.

I want her to clasp her hand to mine, even with the window separating us, but she doesn't. She just looks into my eyes with a complex mix of emotions I cannot decipher.

She holds my gaze and then looks down at the tray with the two small glasses on the table before her.

The Night.

Or the Clear.

I know she can't hear me as I whisper, "I want you to be free of the pain I've caused."

A single tear wells in the corner of her eye. Her arms and shoulders are motionless. Her hands are in her lap below the table.

I watch as the tear runs down her cheek, and I know our love is lost. If we were both to drink the Clear, I would see her turmoil every time I look into her eyes, and I would spend the rest of my life trying to repair the damage I've caused. That's no way for either of us to live.

I remove my hand from the window between us, as if sealing hope in a jar that can never be opened again. I raise the glass of the Clear and stare at it for a moment of time that may be a second or may be forever. The liquid inside moves around and reminds me of a tiny sea. I can almost hear the roar of the ocean's waves crashing against the rocky shoreline.

I lift the Clear and hold it to my lips. It smells like honeysuckle and lavender. I glance once more at Aleah. I feel the Clear touch my lips, which begin to tingle as if from menthol. The taste is sweet with floral undertones followed by heat like pepper. It starts to burn. Tilting the glass back, I drink it all.

For an instant, I feel nothing. I return the empty glass to the tray on the tabletop and lean back in my chair. Then, I feel a glowing, not unpleasant warmth spreading across my chest over my shoulders and down my arms. I look into Aleah's eyes.

The window slowly fades to black, and I can no longer see her. I find myself staring at a heavily tinted black sheet of soundproof glass.

Soon the lights in my cell give way to darkness so complete I can see nothing. The image of a woman's face emerges in the black. She is older, her brow slightly furrowed. Wrinkles line the skin around gray eyes. Her eyebrows are thin. Her silver hair is cut short.

I know this face. It is Aleah's mom.

She is lying in a hospital bed inside a pneumatically sealed chamber. She is dying. Aleah and I stand outside as a gas fills the chamber. Her mother starts coughing blood.

Aleah turns to me and says, "Turn it off! You're killing her! My God, Jordan, what have you done?"

An image of a wide-open field comes toward me in the black. The field lies at the edge of a wooded area. I see a bulldozer and a dump truck working in tandem. The box bed of the truck raises, and bodies pour out onto the ground. The truck pulls away, vanishing into the forest, and the bulldozer starts to push the bodies into a mass grave. I see other dozers in the distance, and I realize the mass grave is enormous, easily a half mile on all sides. Other dump trucks emerge from the woods, then others still.

When I see the pile of corpses inside the grave, it feels like a steel beam slamming into my heart.

"Stop," I say to the darkness. "Make it stop."

The image of a fireplace comes toward me in the black. I feel the heat on my face and hands, and I am sweating. I reach forward and place the newspaper in the blaze, and I watch the paper darken and curl around the photo of Aleah bound by police in the midst of an angry mob. The wood emits a hissing sound in the blaze, and I hear Aleah crying for help as if from the flames.

"What have you done, Jordan?" she says. "I trusted you with everything. Everything!"

Masked demonstrators bang on the black vehicle's windows as Aleah, handcuffed in the backseat, looks out at them.

Other images arise. Too many to count. They're coming at me out of the darkness like a flock of vultures. They press against me on all sides, squeezing my flesh, my bones, my heart. My body shrinks as the images, emotions, and memories of previous lives race toward me.

"Make it stop," I yell.

I see myself standing on a cliff edge in the darkness, rocks and ocean far below, despair weighing on me like an iron vest that just keeps tightening and tightening.

I look down at my certain death below with shame, remorse, and despair of such immense gravity that it squeezes me even more. My feet are at the edge of the cliff. I look down at the rocks far below. I leap out into the air. My arms windmill as I fall. Fear grips me so tightly I stop breathing. I see the waves beating on the rocks, racing toward me. At the moment of impact, a thunderclap rips through the darkness.

As the crack and boom fades, another sound rises, this one carrying all of the voices of my past lives whispering in unison. So many voices speak at once, no single voice is distinguishable from the other. But as the noise grows from hundreds to thousands of voices, the sound starts to resemble that of a waterfall's steady roar, and I wonder if this may be a primordial sound from the birth of the universe.

Awakening

I am face down on a beach. The water from the shoreline reaches my feet and legs, and the sand beneath me is damp and smooth and white as sugar. I hear breakers in the distance and birds chirping and cooing from the forest canopy beyond the beach. I taste sea salt on the back of my throat.

I sit up and look out at a turquoise lagoon in a bay carved into the dark volcanic rock of the island and beyond the lagoon an endless ocean, deep cobalt blue. Only a few clouds spot the sky. The morning sunlight feels warm on my wet skin.

A steady breeze comes in from the sea, rustling the fronds of palm trees that line the beach.

I look down at the remains of a yellow life vest strapped around my chest. My index finger traces over symbols on the lapel.

JOR. V. 3.3

"Jordan," I say. "Version three-point-three."

I remember everything: the last moment I saw Aleah through the glass divide. Drinking the Clear. The memories that came flooding back afterward.

I remember waking alone in a bed in the sub-Los Angeles complex of Anag. Norisis, Inc. and hearing the sound of a clock on the wall. The ticking of the second hand mesmerized me with a clarity and synchrony I was certain came from the source of the universe. I was overcome with a feeling of connectedness to the air that I breathed, to sound waves that carried the vibrations of the machinery inside the clock that my ears received and that my brain processed as this thing we call "sound" and "the ticking of a clock."

I remember realizing for the first time the illusion of separateness. Realizing that time, language, and indeed our perceptions of ourselves *becoming* or *having been* was a mental construct, none of which was real.

And I remember glimpsing the lifetimes my DNA, *my soul* had spent living as a prisoner to my own mind, never knowing this connection to something indefinable and free of language and thought. Science might call it consciousness. Religion, God. But the freedom was in knowing that the words we used to refer to this thing were not the thing itself.

Then I remembered Aleah. And the loneliness of the bed in the underground compound felt like it would swallow me whole. I lay there, remembering our lives together from before the island. The first time I saw her, the joy that she radiated in her smile and in her steady gaze. I remembered how happy she had been during our first few years together, when we were young and in love and the world was ours. The weight of those memories felt like a monolith crushing me on that bed. I became obsessed with memories.

Memories.

In the days that followed, the doctors trained me. "You must not speak of her ever again," they said. "This is the burden of memory. You must learn to let go of the past, even though it will always be with you."

Try as I might, I couldn't let go of the love I felt for her. They might as well have asked me to let go of my arms and legs—or my heart.

"The next stage of human evolution," they said, "requires a deepening connection to consciousness, to presence, to allowing yourself freedom from thought."

I learned the schematics of the lab I'll find on a hillside on this island. I learned about the plants that will nourish me. I learned that they'd decided to keep from me who my collaborator would be. Perhaps, I remember thinking, they are still making up their minds about who it will be.

I kept telling myself, I'll never be able to let her go. I'll never be able to fill the emptiness inside that these memories we shared create in me.

I just wanted her back in my life. I just wanted to touch her, to see her, to gaze into her eyes, to run my fingers through her hair and over her cheek and to cradle her in my arms as our bodies came together.

"It will pass in time," they said. "Your feelings for her. You must channel all that energy into the cure now, Jordan."

And so it was that they prepared me for this island, this new life, where my goal will be to make the world a better place for others for generations to come, to realize this life's potential, to free myself of all self-limiting beliefs, and in so doing, right the mistakes of my previous lives.

•••

Something out of the corner of my eye catches my attention. It is a shape lying on the shoreline perhaps a hundred yards away. How did I not notice it before? I rise to my feet, walking cautiously at first until I realize it is someone.

A woman.

My collaborator.

I begin to run.

She isn't moving. She could be dead. Or newly born from the sea. The water from the lagoon gently rushes up around her body, then recedes back into the turquoise.

The sound of my approach awakens her.

At first, she sits up with one hand in the sand bracing her. She turns to look at the sea and then twists her midsection to gaze inward at the glass structures rising above the treetops on the island's hillside that will be our home. An emotion I cannot quite define informs her posture: her arm looks tense, hand gripped in a fist in the smooth sand, her eyes fixed on the trees beyond the beach. Her pose suggests apprehension at finding herself on the beach. This beach. This island.

Everything about her is familiar. The line of her back, the shape of her head, the way she sits. And when she turns, I stop in my tracks.

I study Aleah's pale green eyes with flecks of brown spotted around the edges, the freckles that speckle her nose. Her full lips are a flat line of calm. I realize she is processing what she's seeing, for I notice the tension eases in her shoulders. I find myself falling to my knees on the sand. The water rushes up around us, then recedes.

She comes to her knees before me, and we gaze into each other's eyes saying nothing.

I have seen it all, how our souls have passed in and out of existence for all eternity. In some lives, we'd meet and recognize each other. In some, we would not.

Since the beginning of time.

And then she raises her hand as if inviting me to put my palm to hers. I press my skin to hers and rejoice as the corners of her mouth tip up in a smile.

Acknowledgements

During the roughest patch in the decade that it took to write this novel, my daughter kept me going. She was a young kid during much of this time, and for a few years she kept asking me every once in a while about how it would end or whether I knew what the ending would be. Without a doubt, it was her asking me with such genuine curiosity that sustained me—despite the voices in my head telling me I should give up and that I don't belong in this world as a writer. So I've dedicated this book to her, and I would like to acknowledge her as the major inspiration.

I've also dedicated this novel to a dear friend who believed in my last novel. He believed in it so much he worked for a decade of his life to make it into a motion picture starring Gabriel Luna and Joanna Vanderham. Thank you, Desmond. You've shaped my life in profoundly positive ways, and I wouldn't be writing this acknowledgement were it not for your belief in me.

I'd also like to acknowledge a group of beta-readers who gave me feedback at various stages over the course of many months. Sherry Mooney, M.R. Pritchard, R.E. Carr, and Danielle Bannister. Your hard work has shaped this novel into a better piece of writing and this writer into a better human being.

I'd like to thank Alan Guthrie for his feedback on drafts around 2017 and 2018, which informed a great deal of the tone and style in earlier versions. I'd also like to thank Megan Sailer who championed *Eddie & Sunny* and whose advice I frequently sought for this novel.

Jordan Version 3.2 wouldn't be published without Kristy Makansi and the team at Blank Slate Press. Kristy, you saw something in this story that gave me hope that maybe it was worthy of putting in front of an audience. Most importantly, you believed in me, and there are no words of gratitude in the human language that can adequately express what this means to me.

Finally, Susan, you've seen me at my best and seen me at my worst, and for some reason, you continue to love me. Over twenty years now. It takes my breath away. You are the inspiration in everything that I do. You are my constant, my everything, my reason, my dream, my antagonist, protagonist, foil, and hero. You are my lover and friend, and I only wish half the people on this planet knew what it feels like to be loved by you. It would improve humanity.

Thank you, all.

—Stacey Cochran, August 5, 2023

About the Author

Stacey Cochran is the author of four previous novels including *Eddie & Sunny*, which was adapted into a major motion picture starring Gabriel Luna and Joanna Vanderham. Stacey was a finalist for the 2011 James Hurst Prize for fiction, a finalist for the 2004 St. Martin's Press/PWA Best First Private Eye Novel Contest, and an Honorable Mention for the *Dell Magazines* Award for Undergraduate Excellence in Science Fiction and Fantasy Writing in 1998. He teaches at the University of Arizona, where he received his Ph.D. in 2022, and he splits his time between homes in Summerhaven and Tucson, Arizona.